FLASHES OF GENIUS
& DRIBBLES OF INSANITY
VOLUME 1

Sam Woodgarth

SAM WOODGARTH

FLASHES OF GENIUS
& DRIBBLES OF INSANITY
VOLUME 1

PAPERBACK ISBN: 978-1-7640098-0-5
EBOOK ISBN: 978-1-7640098-1-2

SAM WOODGARTH
PO BOX 507
TRINITY BEACH
CAIRNS, QUEENSLAND,
4879

Contents

Thought Bubbles

T he grey-black iridescent beads piled up in a corner of the shower stall. Mary first thought they were soap suds, but they didn't dissolve. She poked at them with her toe before picking them up for a closer inspection. Short-sightedly holding them close, she peered at them. Colours swirled inside, slowly revolving, alive and sentient. Startled, Mary dropped them into the sink, where they dulled. She gingerly rinsed them in tepid water. Intrigued, she left them in a saucer and prepared for work.

· · · · · · · · · ·

In the car, she noticed more of the beads. The size of marbles, the colours within writhed. Mary collected them into a pile on the passenger seat. Was it her imagination or did they huddle together?

Mary focused on her driving. She hated driving, or more accurately, she hated other drivers. She considered them all incompetent, while her own skills were masterful. When she parked and glanced at the beads, they seemed to have increased in number, but was that impossible. She scooped them into a discarded grocery bag; they were warm to the touch and almost humming. No sound, but a vibration. Maybe. She tucked the bag out of sight in the footwell. At least they couldn't roll away, the bag kept them secure.

......

Riding the elevator to the seventeenth floor gave Mary the opportunity to appraise her co-workers. None of them were, in her opinion, fit to do the job. Lazy, incompetent, careless and useless. Had she been in charge, she'd have fired them all. She had nothing but contempt for any of them, either above or below her in the company hierarchy.

Stepping out of the elevator, she trod on a bead which silently exploded, releasing a stench like a well-ripened fart. Those remaining cast looks of disgust, but the doors closed before she could explain.

A few beads scattered on the floor by her feet. As she knelt to scoop them up, they rolled towards her like ducklings towards a mother duck. She deposited them gently into her suit jacket pocket.

Mary's workspace was an anonymous cubicle, she didn't merit her own office. If status was accorded to quality and quantity of work, she deserved a corner suite with river views. The imbecile currently inhabiting that space was utterly useless. Mary knew her boss only held his position because he had a half competent Personal Assistant. In Mary's opinion, the PA wasn't worth her salary, either, but she looked the part. Mary mused that creating the right impression was infinitely more important these days than skills or talent.

Her computer went through its interminable setting up processes while Mary carefully hung her suit jacket on a padded hangar, which she hooked over the cubicle wall. Her supervisor bustled towards her, Mary ducked down, maybe she wasn't heading to her specifically. The bloody woman was always complaining about something. Mary would love to tell her what she really thought, but a single woman with a mortgage had to hold her opinions to herself if she wanted to keep her job.

"Mary! Did you step in dog poop on your way in? There's a nasty trail from the lift to here. Call maintenance to send a cleaning crew. God, how can you stand it?" Carol, Mary's supervisor, teetered away on her four-inch heels, holding a hand over her nose.

Automatically, Mary lifted her shoes to check. She couldn't see or smell anything, but she noticed her colleagues stifling smirks. She ran an unmanicured finger down the laminated list of extension numbers and called maintenance. Slamming down the phone, she saw another bead roll lazily across her desk. Colours within writhed and glowed darkly. Mary felt a vibration in her skull. She deftly collected the bead and placed it with the others in her jacket pocket.

The cleaning crew came and went; sullen, rude and inefficient. Mary thought the liberal application of air fresher as they left both unnecessary and impertinent. She fired off an email to the head of maintenance to complain, rather than to thank them for a speedy response.

By lunchtime, Mary had accrued a handful more of the mysterious glowing beads. She slipped them into her pocket as she prepared to leave. Depending on the weather, she ate her lunch either sitting in her car or on a park bench. Today she went directly to her car to add the clutch of beads to the others. The weather was glorious, sunny with a light breeze, too pleasant to huddle in her car. She headed for her usual bench and, as always, she spread a cloth before sitting. *Bloody pigeons crap everywhere. Vermin. That's what they are, bloody vermin. Someone should poison them all! Well, hello. Where did you come from?* Yet another iridescent bead rolled next to Mary, oily colours roiling within. She picked it up and held it between thumb and forefinger. *You really are beautiful, aren't you?* The bead pulsed, and Mary felt the vibration deep in her core. *Bloody pigeons!* The bead pulsed vigorously in response. A bird fell out of the tree, stone dead, startling the others into flight. The bead faded to an inky blackness and stopped pulsating. Dead. Mary frowned as an intriguing thought swam from the murky depths of her mind.

As the pigeons resettled on the nearby branches, Mary closed her eyes and allowed herself, encouraged herself, to think about them. She imagined them spreading filth and disease in their wake, how she wished a civic-minded individual would poison them. Opening her eyes, she saw a fresh scattering of beads. No, not beads. Thought bubbles. These were her thoughts manifest. She concentrated on imagining all the pigeons dying. Flicking her eyes between the birds fluttering to the ground and the thought bubbles dimming in corresponding numbers confirmed her theory. *Bloody Hell!*

Mary jumped to her feet, scattering the dead thought bubbles, and turned to look at her office building. *What if it works on more than pigeons? Will it work on people? Do I have that power?*

Mary intended to punish them all, but her first experiment would be Carol. Carol and her four inch bloody heels. Carol and her effortlessly sleek blond bob; Carol and her shapely legs and trim waist; Carol and her superiority complex that masked her inadequacy. *She really shouldn't have humiliated me this morning. I'll make her pay for that.*

Mary barged her way into an already crowded elevator car, eager to reach the seventeenth floor and test her exciting new theory. She'd bring her down a peg or two. Nothing permanent, just a little humiliation, something to dent her pride.

Mary heard the commotion as soon as the elevator doors slid open. A woman was crying and voices, both male and female, were raised in consternation. A group had gathered around Carol who lay on the floor whimpering.

"Just hold on, sweetheart. Help is on its way, it won't be long. There, there. You'll be alright."

The PA from the corner office had taken charge. She shepherded two of the managers in front of her, instructing them to lift Carol and carry her to the nearest conference room, where they placed her in a comfortably padded chair.

Mary moved to her desk, disappointed to have missed the show but thrilled that her experiment had worked. Carol slipping and spraining an ankle could be a coincidence, but Mary didn't think so. She hugged herself tightly and smiled, before remembering to assume a somber expression. Looking gleeful about Carol's downfall wouldn't be politic.

When she rehung her suit jacket, she found a dead thought bubble in the pocket. It hadn't been there while she ate her lunch, of that she was certain. Once the paramedics had carted Carol away, the afternoon passed slowly. The initial buzz of excitement faded quickly, leaving a void idle gossip couldn't adequately fill.

Mary efficiently emptied her in-tray and worked uninterrupted on her proposal to streamline the department. With Carol away, Mary saw an opportunity to step up the ladder, to demonstrate her efficiency and clarity of vision.

•••••••••

Shrewdly virtuous, Mary packed tomorrow's lunch. Taking a packed lunch had multiple benefits: you didn't pay inflated prices for substandard meals; you used up left-overs, again saving money, but most importantly, you chose where to eat. Mary had eaten in the cafeteria, but had always been uncomfortable. Conversations stuttered when she approached, people no doubt intimidated by her innate superiority. She was much more comfortable eating alone, but that didn't mean she didn't feel the sting of being an outcast. Yeah, the cafeteria crowd. Mary wanted them to experience some of the discomfort they'd inflicted upon her. Mary's eyes widened with pleasure and surprise when a pulsating thought bubble rolled across the kitchen counter to rest next to her lunchbox.

·····•··•····

Mary took longer than usual in the shower, applying conditioner to her hair and shaving her legs, things she usually skipped as unnecessary. She planned to use all possible weapons in her arsenal to impress while Carol was out of commission. If stupid fripperies such as a hair conditioner and lipstick would help win over her idiot bosses, she would use them. By the time she finished, the shower stall was overflowing with vibrating thought bubbles, humming like a nest of exotic insects. Mary carefully gathered each one and placed them in a pile on the countertop. The humming and swirling was hypnotic, only with a great effort did Mary pull herself away.

When she made her bed, she found it infested with thought bubbles. When she held out her hand, they rolled towards her. A few stubbornly inert dead ones turned to odourless ash when she tried to remove them. Before setting out for work, she checked the welfare of the lunchbox thought bubble, which was roiling and pulsating vigorously.

·····•····

No one complimented her more polished appearance, but she caught a few nudges and smirks from the corner of her eye. Mary ignored them. She cleared her in-tray in record time and spent the rest of the morning finessing her proposals. The document was a work of art with colourful charts and graphs to illustrate her ideas.

She watched the first lunch break crew with carefully controlled glee. Upon their return she took her break, choosing to sit again on the pigeon popular bench. There were significantly fewer birds today. Impatient to get back and see the effect of her thought bubble, she was back early to her desk. A sour stench permeated the office, and many desks were empty, with phones left to ring unanswered. Unprecedented. The bossy PA. was not at her post. She was an early luncher. Mary watched with wide-eyed innocence as more personnel left their workstations unattended, some fleeing to different floors when it became clear all the toilets on this floor were occupied – and would be for the foreseeable future.

She watched the lunchbox thought bubble slowly extinguish. Then she called emergency services, reporting a severe case of food poisoning. When the medics arrived, Mary made herself useful to them. It was early evening before anyone not hospitalised was fit enough to travel home. Mary had very much enjoyed herself, being an angel of mercy to her suffering colleagues.

When she eventually packed to leave, the thought bubble had disintegrated to a fine ash, which she easily blew away.

· · · • • · • · · · ·

Mary celebrated her success with canned salmon and ice cream. She rarely indulged in desserts but reasoned she deserved a treat and tomorrow was shaping up to be a big day.

· · · • • · • · · · ·

As Mary anticipated, few staff turned up for work. She went straight to the directors and informed them she would hire a few dozen temps for the next week or so, to at least keep things ticking over. Relieved someone was taking charge, they gave her carte blanche to do as she saw fit. She may not have been popular, but everyone knew she was efficient and company oriented. For the next week, Mary was in heaven. The temps deferred to her and the bosses were grateful. This is how her life ought to be. Finally, after years of service, she was being recognised and appreciated.

Then Carol came back. On crutches! Fearless and determined, Carol to the rescue. A woman on crutches. Everyone, directors and temps, thought she was a saint. You can't expect someone on crutches to do anything, so everyone fluttered around her, making sure she was comfortable and constantly caffeinated. Carol had the temerity to appropriate Mary's best temp as her own PA. Speechless with barely suppressed fury, Mary sat in her cubicle among a rapidly growing collection of threateningly iridescent thought bubbles. They swarmed around her ankles and across her keyboard, increasingly animated. Now Carol was back, Mary was invisible again.

· · · • • · • · · · ·

Each night, the thought bubbles swarmed in Mary's bed, warming her. The lullaby of their chitinous quivering sent her to sleep, but she awoke tired each morning. Everyone noticed how she appeared aged in the last weeks. They attributed the premature ageing to stress. Carol, the directors and the temps all gossiped and agreed Mary wasn't coping with the extra responsibilities. Her work was still exemplary, but physically Mary was deteriorating. Her skin was fragile and papery, her hair brittle and streaked with grey. She lost weight, too. Never voluptuous, she was now skeletal. Blue veins showed on the backs of her hands. Mary saw the changes in herself and they fuelled her fury. All she had sacrificed for the company and still they refused to recognise her value.

·•·•·•·•·•·

Mary considered herself a fair and generous person, and a good neighbour. She didn't speak to her neighbours, that's how good she was, no bother at all. The man who lived next door wasn't such a great neighbour. He had his television on full volume while he cheered for his football team. She heard several voices, he must have friends over. *Inconsiderate bastards!*

Mary stomped around to her neighbour's and battered on the door. Her beer soused neighbour leaned on the jamb for support.

"I'm from next door, you're making my life impossible. I want you to turn down the sound on your television. And stop screaming and shouting. You do know the players can't hear you?" Mary leaned forward and stared him right in the eyes, daring him to defy her.

"Next door?" The swaying man squinted to bring Mary into focus. "Riiiiight! You must be Mary's mum! Come on in, join us, have a beer. Bring Mary - we've plenty of beer."

Humiliated and speechless, Mary turned to flee. Thought bubbles spilled incontinently from her pockets.

"Hey, lady! You're losing your marbles!" Giggling helplessly at his own humour, the neighbour staggered back to his guests.

Tears of frustration and humiliation cascaded down Mary's withered cheeks. To have her complaint ignored as though it was of no consequence! But to be mistaken for her own mother! Physical vanity was not one of Mary's vices, but this rapid ageing horrified her.

Back in the security of her own kitchen, she heard the whoops and cheers continuing from next door and convinced herself the laughter was at her expense. How dare they ignore her request and how dare they laugh at her? She should have stayed, insisted he turn down the volume. Mary seethed and fumed at her impotence. Both colleagues and neighbours ignored her. There must be something she could do to teach him a lesson. All she'd asked him to do was to turn down the damned television.

Running the thought bubbles through her gnarled fingers, she took comfort from their hum and swirling colours. Their agitation increased with hers; they drew her in, mesmerising her.

A crash from next door broke the spell. Mary cocked her head, listening intently. No television, just male voices arguing. Mary smiled to herself. Quiet at last. The thought bubbles ceased to agitate and faded. She left them on the countertop to disintegrate with dignity. The hesitant knock on the door startled her. This was the first time anyone had knocked on her door. She considered ignoring it, but curiosity won out. The neighbour and his football fan friends had arrayed themselves outside her door, bearing cartons of beer and plundered pizza boxes.

"Missus, we wondered if we could move the party here. It's the final and the telly just fell off the wall. Please?"

Several of the friends mutely offered the beer and pizza.

"Your television fell off the wall? That was the crash I heard?"

"Yes, ma'am."

Mary threw back her head and roared her delight.

"Ma'am?"

"Fuck off!" Mary slammed the door on their astonished faces. *Damn! That felt good.*

Back in the kitchen, Mary swept the thought bubble dust into the sink and watched it swirl down the drain. Peace and quiet, with recognition of her power reestablished.

As Mary lay in her bed, thought bubbles multiplied around her, their susurrations lulling her to sleep. She dreamed of bringing low her supercilious colleagues, of standing above them, alone and victorious.

She awoke weary, emaciated and colourless. Swollen joints made moving slow and painful. Peering bleary eyed into the bathroom mirror, Mary's physical deterioration shocked her. A chill of horror replaced the euphoria from the previous evening.

·········

Mary's appearance appalled Carol. She came straight over to Mary's cubicle and crouched next to her, pushing the crutches to one side. Mary was panting with the exertion of getting from her car to the lift, then from the lift to her workstation. She knitted together her fingers to stop them trembling.

"Oh Mary, you really shouldn't be here. You should be at home … or in hospital."

Mary wordlessly shook her head, too breathless to speak. *Carol just wants to get rid of me. She doesn't really care about my wellbeing; it's just an act. She wants everyone to see how selfless she is, coming to work on crutches, being a martyr.*

"Don't argue, Mary. It's decided. We'll get you home, call a doctor, and you can concentrate on getting well again. Rest, that's what you need, poor thing. Just give me a few minutes to get everything arranged, okay?"

Mary sat at her computer, too exhausted to switch it on. She closed her eyes and leaned back to await Carol's return. Mary determined to turn this to her advantage, to bring down Carol and the idiot bosses.

Carol returned with one of the maintenance crew in tow. She put out her hand.

"I need your car keys. You're not fit to drive, goodness only knows how you got here. Anyway, I'll drive you home and Jimmy here will follow in your car. That way, you won't feel trapped." Carol smiled brightly. "Okay? Keys, please."

Mary nodded toward her handbag.

"In there, keys are in there. Thank you. It's very good of you to take care of me like this."

Jimmy and Carol helped Mary to the lift and then to Carol's car, where they strapped her in for the silent ride home.

"Lucky I drive an automatic, I'd be buggered in a manual, what with this ankle."

Mary looked sideways at Carol, but otherwise didn't respond.

Jimmy carefully parked Mary's car, then helped Carol get the invalid into the house. Carol noticed it was immaculate, except for random piles of fine charcoal coloured powder on saucers and plates. Was Mary doing drugs? Did that explain her unusual decline? Concerned for Mary's welfare, Carol snuck a peek in the fridge, thankful to see it was well stocked. She shooed Jimmy outside to wait while she made Mary as comfortable as possible.

Carol herded Mary into the bedroom with instructions to get into bed. Minutes later, she came in with a tray. She'd made a plate of sandwiches and a thermos of coffee. She put Mary's phone next to the thermos.

"You've been neglecting yourself, Mary. Make sure you eat something. And call the doctor. Or would you like me to call now? It's no trouble."

Mary moaned and shook her head. Carol's ministrations irritated her. *Who the hell does she think she is, taking charge like this, pretending to care, so she'll look good to the bosses. Bitch.* Mary fluttered a hand in dismissal.

"I'll call you tomorrow, Friday, to see how you're doing, okay? You've worked yourself into the ground, Mary, but you must rest now, put yourself first, okay? Right, well, I'll call tomorrow. Just call me if there's anything you need, okay?"

Mary closed her eyes while Carol backed awkwardly out of the room. Mary listened for the snick of the front door closing and the purr of Carol's car driving away.

· · • • · • • · · ·

"Jimmy, did you notice anything strange in Mary's home?"

"Strange? No, I don't think so ... unless you mean it was freakishly tidy, like a show home, not a proper home ... and those random piles of ash she keeps in saucers. That's kinda weird."

"You noticed them too? You don't think Mary's … well … do you think the ash could be … ?" Carol faltered, unable to suggest Mary might be doing something illegal and dangerous.

Jimmy sniggered.

"You suggesting miserable Mary's getting high on illicit substances, Carol? Nah, I don't think so. Looked to me more like she was burning incense; everyone's talking about how she's running herself into the ground. Maybe she's trying to meditate and relax."

"You're so right, it was incense! Silly me! That's such a relief."

True to her word, Carol rang the following afternoon. Too exhausted to say much, Mary promised, at Carol's urging, to look after herself. If anything, Mary felt weaker. Angrier, too. *Carol's an interfering busybody who needs bringing down.*

· · · ● · ● · · ·

Mary's temps left on time on Friday, full of praise for Carol's compassionate management. Not only had she been kind to miserable Mary, but she'd secured contracts for most of them, either fixed term or permanent, to replace those who were recovering or had died from the mystery food poisoning.

Carol and the bosses had lingered before deciding to meet up in the bar across the road. They all crowded into the same elevator, continuing the conversation about Mary's impressive proposals. They had decided to promote her and give her a private office space on her return to work. This meeting in the bar was an early celebration. Carol planned to phone Mary over the weekend and share the good news. She hoped it would speed Mary's recovery.

The lift clanged to a grinding halt between floors. The lights flickered out, and the conversation faltered to a stop. Carol shone her phone torch towards the control panel.

"Press the emergency button, someone will come soon."

The wail of the emergency siren competed with stifled screams as the car plummeted a short distance. Loud metallic groans and creaks struck fear in everyone's heart. The lift jerked again. Carol and her companions lurched wildly, grabbing onto one another.

"Hello, lift number two! This is Jimmy from maintenance. Who's there? Is there a problem?"

"Jimmy? Jimmy, it's me, Carol, from yesterday. Hi, yeah, we've got a problem. Our lift is stuck … it's dropped a couple of times, but now it's stuck again. Can you help us?"

· · · • · • • · · ·

Mary's sleep was far from restful. Claustrophobia grabbed her by the throat, she pushed away the covers and gasped for air. She felt trapped; she couldn't see but she could hear her own panicked breathing. The darkness swirled around her, a vicious entity, seeking fresh victims. Mary's heart raced, then crashed to a stop. The thought bubbles swelled before losing animation. Mary's terror filled dead eyes stared into the darkness. Thought bubble dust formed her shroud.

· · • • · • • · · ·

"Okay, Carol, I need you to stay calm for me. It'd be easier for everyone if you could turn off the alarm. Can you do that? Pull the emergency button back out."

A white-faced man nearest the panel fumbled in the dark, found the button and yanked hard. The ensuing silence was a balm. He smiled in the dark and nodded in Carol's direction.

"Well done guys, that's better. Okay then, the fire crew've arrived ahead of the elevator techs. They've shut down the power so your car won't move now. You're all doing okay, right? Right. We need to know how many of you are in there."

"Erm, hold on, let me double check. Okay, guys? Call out you names so I can get a number for the firemen."

Including herself, there were seven people trapped in the elevator. Carol reported the numbers back to Jimmy, who kept up a comforting rumble of conversation, keeping everyone calm.

"You're gonna hear someone thumping around up there shortly. The firies are gonna locate exactly where you are, we need to know which floor you're closest to, to decide the best way to get you all out. Hang on a sec, someone's telling me … yeah … okay … Carol? Carol, yeah, I'm back. Okay, right, we know exactly where you are now. You're gonna hear a lot of noise, it's okay, someone will enter the shaft above you and open the access panel in the car's ceiling. It'll be noisy, but you're all quite safe, okay?"

"Okay, Jimmy. Thanks. We can hear them!"

Although expected, the thumping and grinding were still nerve-wracking. A torch-lit face appeared, grinning above them. Seven breaths were expelled simultaneously.

"You must be Carol. Hi, I'm Ben. Behind me here is John. I'm coming in, make some room, I'll help you put on a harness and John will hoist you up and help you to the floor above. Dave will help you out into the lobby. All you guys have to do is follow our instructions. You'll be out in no time." Ben grinned again and lowered himself into the car.

"Ladies first."

Ben strapped a harness under Carol's arms and lifted her up to the access door. John took up the slack and hauled her up and out of sight. The men could hear multiple voices, there was an entire team helping them. One by one, they donned the harness, and John hauled them to safety. By the time Ben surfaced, everyone was slumped against the lobby walls or sitting on the floor. Jimmy from maintenance had rustled up a tray of coffees.

"Lady and gentlemen, gather your belongings, we've eight flights of stairs to get down. It makes my job much easier if you can all stay together."

"Eight flights? Sir, I don't think Carol can manage that. She sprained her ankle …"

"Well Carol, we can put you on a stretcher, no problem, or we could carry you?"

Blushing furiously, Carol protested she'd be fine and refused any assistance. Ben stayed close beside her all the way, allowing her to set the pace. When they reached the foyer, they noticed the Out-of-Order sign on lift number two and the small team of technicians who had arrived to fix the fault. Everyone spread out and milled around aimlessly, unsure what to do next.

"Are we still on? The bar's open and I could really use a drink," said Carol.

Everyone flocked to her, grateful she had voiced their thoughts. Once settled in the bar, the conversation inevitably returned to Mary. Everyone agreed when she came back to work, they'd have a proper celebration. Her proposals had impressed everyone and it would be to the company's advantage to make better use of her skills.

Ben barged into the bar, head turning frantically to find Carol. He called her name, and she waved. People moved out of his way, clearing a path between them.

"We found these in the elevator and the stairs. You must've snapped the string getting out of the elevator." He thrust a handful of beautiful pearlescent beads at her. They appeared to pulse and hum.

"But … they're not mine."

Ben looked at the pearly beads, then at Carol.

"I think they must be yours, look," he nudged a solitary bead next to Carol's glass. "See? You lost another one. They obviously belong to you."

Previously published: The Holes in Everything & Other Stories

2019

Barbecue

"Well, that was disappointing, not even remotely scary." Anna zapped the remote at the giant wall-mounted television and slumped back on the oversized leather sofa. "Seriously, who's stupid enough to go out in a storm, wearing only their skimpiest underwear, to investigate strange noises? Idiots deserve decapitating!"

"You say that every time." Bella waggled her wine glass. "Anyone fancy a refill?"

"Not for me. I'm starving," Cassie said. "When are the boys delivering dinner?"

"Shush, I hear it coming." Anna put a finger to her blood-red lips.

The cabin door crashed open. A frenzied wind howled into the large cabin, making the candle flames shiver and gutter. Misshapen shadows danced on colourful wall hangings. A power cut threw the cabin into semi-darkness. The trio smiled in anticipation.

"Help! Anyone home? Help us, please!" Two young men hesitated on the threshold, rivulets of stormwater puddling around their boots. Backlit by the storm, their features were unidentifiable, but they were tall and well built. They were also bloody, the bearded one supporting his injured companion.

The sisters glided closer. The exhausted men breathed heavily. Blood from myriad cuts and grazes combined with terror sweat to form a powerful primal cologne.

Annie raised a candle. "Oh, my goodness! Look at you!"

"What happened? Were you in an accident?" Bella's nostrils flared.

"Come." Cassie gestured for them to enter.

As Anna and Bella helped the men onto the sofas, they inhaled their intoxicating scents. Cassie closed the door, and then dashed upstairs for supplies. The wind howled like an enraged beast denied its rightful prey. Gusts buffeted roof and windows, and screeched down the chimney, scattering sparks onto the handmade rug, which, barefoot, Bella stomped out without flinching.

"Police … we need the police," gasped the man with the injured leg. Red hair clung in wet clumps to his skull and his green eyes swam with tears. "Please, call the police."

"It's all right, Harry. I don't think they followed us this far. We're safe now, bro'."

Cassie returned with an armful of faded clothes and fresh towels. She tossed a pile of sweats and flannel shirts onto the table. "You fellas want to dry off and get changed? Bathroom's through there." She pointed. "Can you manage?"

"Tom, can you help me up? My ankle won't take my weight …"

Tom hauled Harry to his feet, calling the trio's attention to his smoothly rippling muscles under his drenched shirt. Tom draped Harry's arm over his shoulders and they hobbled to the bathroom.

Bella scooped up the pile of clothes and towels.

"I'll bring these for you." She skipped ahead of them into the bathroom. "There's enough hot water for you both to wash up."

With the men busy in the bathroom, the trio sprang into action.

Anna collected the first-aide kit and a dusty bottle of brandy older than herself. Bella fetched two bowls of hot water and more towels.

Cassie unplugged the landline and flipped the switches on the power box. "You can't be too careful. Don't want power back until we're ready."

"Anna, your people have outdone themselves this year," said Cassie. "Two! They smell delicious! My tummy's rumbling! We must do something nice in return."

Anna smirked. "We never 'must' do anything for the villagers, don't forget that. The peasants owe us their lives. If we do something nice, it's because we choose to demonstrate our magnanimity."

The men emerged from the steamy bathroom, pink skinned and glowing. Tom lowered Harry onto the nearest sofa.

"Thanks ladies, it's kind of you to let two strangers into your home at night. I'm Tom and this is my brother, Harry. We're grateful for your hospitality."

"You don't look like much of a threat," Anna said. "Couldn't exactly send you away now, could we? What sort of monsters would send injured men into a thunderstorm?"

As if to prove her point, lightning lit the surrounding woods in stark relief, another round of thunder rolled and crashed, and the vibrations shook dust from the rafters.

"I'm Anna, these are my sisters, Bella and Cassie. What happened, you said someone attacked you ...?"

"Uh, yeah, any chance I could use your phone? There's a bunch of gun-toting crazies out there," Tom jabbed with his thumb. "You should lock the door. They know where we are."

Bella handed the phone to Tom.

"I can't get any service. Damn. We didn't bring our phones. Knew we'd be out of reception while we were hiking. Didn't want to be disturbed, either."

"Storms frequently bring down the phone lines." Bella shrugged. "The electricity is off, too; lucky we have candles. Happens a lot, up here, but we're prepared. Looks like you're stuck for the night. Why don't you tell us your story while we dress your wounds? My, but that's a nasty cut!" Bella licked her lips as she bent to apply a dressing.

Anna pulled the cork, and a rich fruity aroma swirled through the cabin. "This'll help blunt the pain. I'm told it's good for shock, too."

Tom and Harry quaffed the brandy, and Anna immediately refilled their glasses. "So, what happened?"

"Well, we were hiking the trail, planning to camp overnight. We needed to get out of town for a couple of days, clear our heads, didn't we, Harry?"

"Yeah, it was spur-of-the-moment. We needed a fresh perspective, y'know?"

"Really? A fresh perspective? On what?" Anna distracted the men while Cassie and Bella dressed the superficial cuts and grazes before moving on to Harry's injured leg.

"Yeah, well, it's embarrassing. I just lost a huge contract and I don't know if my business will survive. If I don't have to shut up shop, I'll at least have to lose some staff. I hate to let people go, especially at this time of year. I thought the mountain air might help clear my head, find a solution."

"Yeah … horrible to terminate people right before the holidays." Harry teared up again. "My girlfriend dumped me. I didn't see it coming, I planned to propose this weekend. Bought the ring, booked her favourite restaurant, everything. How stupid do I feel? Thought some bro' time might help."

"And it was going well, right until this storm blew up."

"Yeah, the storm and the crazies arrived together," Harry said. "They must've followed us, maybe from the car park … or maybe from when we stopped in the village to stock up on snacks …"

"Yeah, we thought we were being followed, kept seeing things, but not really … whoever they were, they stayed out of sight. We called out, but no one answered."

"Not at first, no, but when it started raining, they hurled stones at us. We thought it was hail at first, weren't too worried until one of them fired a gun and the pelting stones got worse."

"Scared the heck out of us both. We dropped our packs and ran, and that's when Harry fell, twisted his ankle, really slowed us down."

"Yeah, that was weird, because Tom was almost carrying me, and we couldn't escape, but they didn't come closer. They kept up a barrage of pebbles and stones with the occasional gunshot, kept us moving, herded us along until we stumbled onto this track …"

"Yeah, they must've known you ladies live here, because they backed off. We heard them crashing about, even in the storm, like they wanted us to know they were there, all around us, but when we saw your lights, they faded away."

"Don't think I've ever been so scared in my entire life, don't mind admitting it, either. Kept hearing Duelling Banjos playing in my head."

The brandy took its inevitable effect. The trio scrutinised Tom and Harry as they nodded off and jerked awake.

"Sandwiches? Soup? We can heat soup on the gas stove. You boys should eat, then get some rest." Anna said as she pulled Bella and Cassie into the kitchen. "We'll only be a moment."

"What do you think?" Anna asked as she sharpened the carving knife on a well-worn whetstone.

"Doesn't sound like anyone knows they're here and they've both suffered unexpected setbacks. Won't surprise anyone if they don't come back. I think they're perfect." Cassie sprinkled the soup with her special concoction of soporific herbs.

"Only issue I can see is the car," Bella said. "Cassie, you know who to call, arrange someone to check it out, then dump it in a ravine."

"I'm on it." Cassie pulled her mobile from her pocket and stepped into the pantry for privacy, an extra precaution. "All taken care of," she said as she re-entered the kitchen a few moments later. "Ready to feed the livestock?" She nodded at the trays. "Supper!" She held the door for Anna and Bella, who carried trays laden with hot vegetable soup and freshly cut sandwiches.

Tom and Harry hoed into the food before recalling their manners.

"Oops! Are you ladies not eating?" Shamefaced, Tom pushed the remaining sandwiches towards the girls.

"No, we'll feed later, eat up." Anna pushed the plate back, her curled lips barely covering her gleaming teeth.

The combination of heat from the fire, food, and expensive brandy made Tom and Harry's heads droop again.

"Okay, boys, off to bed. You can share the room at the back, where you won't have to tackle the stairs." Anna led the way with spare candles, Bella supported Harry, and Cassie guided tipsy Tom.

"Ensuite's through there. See you in the morning." Anna turned down the homemade quilt to reveal dazzling white sheets.

Tom and Harry barely made it under the covers before they succumbed to oblivion.

The sisters gathered before the fireplace, their eyes reflected the red glow of the embers.

"Well, girls? Verdict, please?" Anna beamed at Bella and Cassie.

"Excellent condition, young, healthy, no obvious diseases. They can marinade overnight," Bella said.

Cassie's mobile trilled. She raised a finger before she answered. "Are you sure? You've double checked? And all social media? Well done! Excellent job … just a second …" Cassie put her caller on hold.

"My verdict? I agree one-hundred percent with Bella, and our boys have disposed of the car and the discarded backpacks. The ID found in the car confirmed their story. The car, an older model with no tracking device, belonged to Tom. No phones tucked away. It's been double and triple checked; no surviving relatives, social media confirmed Tom and Harry have few personal connections and they didn't advertise their spur-of-the-moment plans. They were considerate enough to pay for their snacks with cash, too. All good."

"Great," Anna said. "Since the hunters chose so well and there'll be enough to share, invite the boys for a barbecue tomorrow. Let's make it a real Halloween party!"

Cassie turned back to her phone. "Hi, you still there? Yeah, you did good. My sisters and I would like to show our appreciation. How about you and the boys come over tomorrow afternoon for a barbecue? We've two prime bucks, so plenty of meat."

Trick or Treat

Mel parked her battered jalopy in the usual spot and stared at the tattered neon poster pasted across the window of Treasures & Tea Leaves.

Closing Down Sale!

I'd better make this one count. She pushed through the door, oddly relieved the jangling chimes still greeted her. The odour of lavender furniture polish and industrial strength disinfectant combined in a familiar mélange. Dust motes swirled a languid dance in hazy beams of sunlight.

Kathy, with her blue-rinsed wedge haircut, unchanged since 1976, greeted her with a rueful smile. "I hoped you'd come. Today's my last trading day, so everything's half-price. I'll put the kettle on while you browse." She bustled into the back room to put together a tray for her favourite customer.

Mel wandered between teetering piles of unwanted crockery, racks of outdated clothing, and sets of mismatched chairs. Baskets of brooches and beads cluttered the counter. Cheap tat, suitable for children's dress-up boxes or fancy-dress outfits. She tipped out a basket of bracelets and lurid plastic necklaces and finger-raked them over the glass counter. More than once, she'd happened upon authentic art déco Lucite pieces jumbled among the rubbish, and resold them on online for hefty profits.

A giant sparkly spider brooch caught her attention. Figurative jewellery enjoyed waves of popularity, but usually cute cats and dogs, pretty enamelled birds and butterflies, even bees. But not spiders. Few women choose to have an arachnid crawling over their collar or creeping along their hat brims.

Mel whipped out her loupe to inspect the spider, whose articulated legs spanned her palm. *Surely not?* She schooled her face into a mask of indifference and shoved a few random paste rings into an untidy heap.

Kathy returned with a tray of pretty but disparate Royal Doulton, a plate of chocolate biscuits, and a pot of lapsing souchong, which she eased onto the counter.

"Are you relocating?"

Kathy shook her head. "Increased rents and online shopping are driving me out. I've tried listing things on the internet but it's beyond me. I don't understand how it works. Time to put my feet up, make way for the youngsters like you who do everything thing differently." She pushed a cup towards Mel and proffered the plate of biscuits.

"Thanks. What will happen to all this stuff?" Mel gestured with her bourbon cream to encompass the store.

"I've got a man coming tomorrow." Kathy wiped a tear. "He usually does house clearance, estate stuff, but he's promised to take everything, a job lot. Saves me messing about."

"I could help you put some smaller items online. Things you can send via the post."

"That's sweet of you, but it's time to retire. I'm too old to learn these newfangled ways." Kathy tapped her chest. "This is a blessing, really. My doctor says there's nothing they can do. I haven't much time left. He says I need to take things easy. I'm going to concentrate on my orchids."

"I'm sorry to hear that." Mel brushed off her crumbs, gathered the tangled strings of beads and returned them to the basket. She pointed to the pile of rings and brooches. "I'll take these. The spider will be a fun Halloween piece."

Kathy rummaged under the counter for tissue paper and gift bags. Her arthritic fingers fumbled as she carefully wrapped each item. She left the spider until last. "I've a box for this somewhere." She ducked below the counter and emerged with a triumphant smile and a forest-green box embossed with a flamboyant gold crest. "Must have been a promotion gift. Faberge for Men aftershave. All the rage in my day. Between you and me, the stuff stank like a tart's boudoir. Can't quite see the connection between creepy crawlies and aftershave, though."

Mel winced as Kathy scratched an imagined flaw on the box before laying the spider on its bed of ivory satin.

"What do I owe you?" Mel asked.

Kathy wrinkled her nose. "Call it a goodbye present. You've been my favourite customer."

"But you need the money."

"A couple of dollars isn't going to impact my retirement. Think of me when you're trick-or-treating. Let me read your leaves one last time."

Mel swirled the dregs of her tea and turned the cup upside down on the saucer.

Kathy peered into the cup, as she had every Friday afternoon for the last two years. A shadow of a frown crossed her face, immediately replaced with a sunny smile. "Hmm. I still don't see Mr Tall Dark and Handsome, but I do see unexpected good fortune. Yes, very soon."

Mel bit her tongue and picked up the gift bag. *How can Kathy not see what's right under her nose? If I gave her a piece of porcelain, she'd tell me which pottery produced it and when, whether it was a transfer or hand painted, and if so, by which artist, but she's blind to jewellery.* "Thanks, again. See you around." She hurried out of the shop, certain her flaming cheeks would betray her.

Mel shivered under thunderous skies, and a spatter of fat raindrops prompted her to hurry. She placed the gift bag in the glove compartment. Her car started on only the second attempt. She weaved through rain-slashed streets to the unscrupulous but high-end jeweller who had bought previous pieces. Rain drummed on the car roof, silvery puddles overflowed over the car park and gurgled down greedy drains.

Mel opened the boxed spider and rechecked the hallmark. Lack of paperwork would impact the value, but this was the find of a lifetime. She returned the brooch to the box and pushed it to the bottom of her bag before checking her lipstick in the rear-view mirror. *Don't want to look shabby. This deal is too important.* She locked the car door and jiggled the handle. *Can't be too careful.*

She pressed the doorbell and smiled at the security camera. A buzz invited her into the plushly carpeted establishment. *Too upmarket for a mere shop.*

"Miss Taylor, what improbable treasures do you have for me today?" The tall, thin man with a pointed chin always reminded Mel of a praying mantis. He ushered her to a side table flanked by two Louis XV chairs and laid a velvet tray on the tiny tabletop.

Genuine antiques or expensive reproduction? She dug into her bag. "This is special, Mr King. I think a man of your caliber will appreciate the quality." She placed the box on the tray.

Mr King smiled his professionally neutral smile as he opened the embossed leather lid. "Gracious." He glanced at Mel as he picked up his loupe. His fingers trembled as he examined the spider. "Not your usual fare, Miss Taylor. Do you know what this is?"

"I'd like your confirmation."

Mr King sucked his lip as he re-examined the hallmark and double checked the stones. In silence, he consulted a manual, then skimmed the local police report of stolen items, genteelly concealed in a soft suede folder.

"Well? What do you think?"

"May I inquire how this came into your possession?"

"A present. For Halloween." Mel nodded at the photocopied report. "I didn't steal it."

"Somebody must think a great deal about you to give you such a generous gift."

"Maybe, but I'd prefer cash. Are you going to make an offer?"

"There's a very limited market for figural brooches featuring insects." Mr King simpered.

"Fortunate for us it's an arachnid, not an insect. And we both know there's a vast market, local and international, for items of this quality." Mel held out her hand. "Of course, if it's beyond your capacity, I can auction it online."

"I don't suppose you have any paperwork to prove provenance?"

Mel shook her head.

"Pity. That affects the value." He squinted. "How much are you asking?"

"What are you offering?"

He pursed thin lips. "Without provenance … six thousand."

Mel held out her hand and smiled sweetly. "Not even close, Mr King. A platinum brooch of this size, encrusted with diamonds and rubies? Then, when you add in the Faberge name?

Carl Faberge? The main man?" Mel raised her eyebrows. "Takes it to a different level, wouldn't you agree, Mr King?"

"You knew it was Carl Faberge?" Mr King slumped.

"I'm not a rube, Mr King, and I'm insulted you tried to cheat me. I thought we shared mutual respect. Incy Wincy and I will go elsewhere."

"How much will you accept?" Mr King's eyes glittered hard as diamonds.

"At auction, I'd expect to get an easy eighty thousand, but I'm not unreasonable. You got to make a profit, too. Fifty-five is my lowest number."

"At the right auction, it might sell for seventy-five. Take off 30 percent fees, that leaves me slightly over fifty. I'm taking the financial risk, Miss Taylor. I'll give you twenty thousand."

Mel shook her head. "Forty-five."

"You're being unreasonable. I could have my investment tied up for years until the right buyer surfaces."

"I could sell it privately." *Which I'm certain you'll do. You have the connections.*

"Indeed, you could. But you might wait five or ten years for a suitable prospect. Or you could take thirty thousand now. No risk to yourself."

"Thirty-five."

"Very well, thirty-five thousand." Mr King sighed heavily as he prepared the paperwork and counted out the cash. "Are you sure you wouldn't prefer an electronic transfer? This is a lot of cash to carry around, Miss Taylor."

Mel stuffed the bundles into her bag. "I trust cash." She splashed to the car through the pelting rain, locked herself in, and clutched the bag to her chest.

Thirty-five big ones!

The car rattled and died. Mel closed her eyes and turned the key again. The engine shuddered and coughed back to life. *I can afford a new car? I could pay off my student loans?*
Or go halves with Kathy?

Previously published: After Dinner Conversation

January 2023

Dazzled

Peering through the gym window, I goggle slack-jawed at our instructor hanging upside down by sheer willpower. Or superglue. I have no idea how she's attached to that pole, but I know I'll never master her technique.

For a start, she weighs about twenty percent of my body weight. And most of that is from the holographic spangles on her impossibly tiny thong bikini. Do they even manufacture poles to support my Rubenesque curves?

As a newly single woman, I've become a pet project for my work colleagues. My connubial happiness has become their mission. What they fail to understand, cannot and will not understand, is that I've never been happier. Being out of condition - okay, fat - isn't an issue for me. I honestly don't care that I have lumpy, bumpy bits. Being single is fan-freaking-tastic! I answer to no one. For the first time ever, I'm free to do what I want, when I want, and only bloody well if I want.

Last week, Linda had looked pityingly at the contents my shopping trolley. "Is this really the way you want to live? Frozen meals for one and family sized chocolate cakes?"

"Hell, yeah!"

She'd tutted and shook her head. "You're saying that now, but I know you don't mean it. Not deep down. Not in your heart."

Linda assumed the fervid expression she always wears when she takes on a new project and I quailed. Linda is a juggernaut of good intentions, and she'll bulldoze you into submission with her frequent but usually short-lived enthusiasms. Her history is littered with squashed and abandoned relationships and objects, but true to form, she refuses to notice. Always the next new shiny object to pursue in her exhausting and never ending safari to bag a personal fulfilment trophy.

My colleagues' only conception of fulfilment is framed in terms of being size zero, and snagging a man. A young, good-looking one is preferable, but I suspect in my case they may lower their expectations to "still breathing". Possibly one foot in the grave and the other on a banana skin.

I watch, hypnotised, as the teacher spins around, contorting her pipe-cleaner carcass in ways not only unnatural, but make me dizzy. The eye-stabbing glare from her holographic sequins threatens to give me a migraine.

"Let's do an exotic dance class," they said. "It'll be fun," they said.

I need to check the dictionary, because this looks as far removed from my idea of fun as it's possible to get. This is torture. I'm willing to bet there's a stern mention of this in the UN Charter of Human Rights.

My workmates have shed their office attire and are wearing … not much, except their lip gloss smiles.

"You can't wear a track suit. You won't be able to grip the pole … between your thighs," giggles the blonde with the high-set ponytail, blushing like a schoolgirl.

Linda drags me to the exercise-wear shop in the foyer. The stick-insect behind the counter offers a twisted smile when Linda explains my predicament. Looks more like a sneer, but could be the Botox doing its toxic thing. But that's all she offers. They don't stock my size. She'd have to make phone calls, see if she can locate "something suitable". The skinny bitch actually makes air quotes.

"I'll sit this one out. You can tell me all about it." As soon as they slip into the torture chamber, I rummage in my bag. It's still there. A bacon, lettuce, and tomato sandwich left over from lunch. Moaning with pleasure, I look up to see a chunky janitor wielding a broom, and frowning at my snack.

I blush and stuff my late lunch back into its cellophane wrapper. "Sorry. Wasn't thinking. Didn't mean to drop crumbs. I'll take it outside."

The janitor raises a thick, untamed eyebrow. "Missed lunch, eh? A gorgeous goddess like you deserves more than that miserable offering. Fancy coming for pizza? Great place around the corner, cheese crust, deep pan, double everything."

I shimmy to the door and wink over my shoulder. "And a wicked dessert to finish?"

Beer Goggles

My world spins as I watch from across the room. A corona of stars swirls around her head. She walks on rainbows. *Is this love?*

The universe revolves around this woman. People gravitate to her, but she pushes them away. She's noticed me. This glorious creature, a goddess, glides towards me.

"I haven't seen you here before." Her voice chimes like silver bells.

"No. This is my first time." I blush at the banal immaturity of my words, and my stomach gurgles with ominous urgency.

My angel smiles. "You should pace yourself." She drifts away on golden clouds, the gravitational centre of the party.

Music thunders and my innards cramp. I race to the back door and lose myself in an overgrown garden. Once my belly is empty, I lie looking at the stars.

I wake to the clatter of bottles tipping into the recycling bin. My skull reverberates like a tribal timpani. I moan like a sick cat and haul myself to my uncoordinated feet. A chill breeze wafts the odour of vomit and my stomach responds. I lean over, hands on knees to dry retch.

"Feeling better?" Her voice claws behind my eyeballs and I wince. "I'm doing a fry-up in a few minutes, if you can walk as far as the breakfast bar." She oozes cynical amusement.

I rub crusty gunk from the corners of my eyes and squint. My goddess has reassumed mortal form. Sausage thighs encased in stretchy denim. The bulging, wobbly shape of my best friend's mum. More Venus of Willendorf than Botticelli's blonde bombshell.

Alcohol? Never again.

Until next weekend.

A Date with Death

F riday evening, I arrived home frazzled, threw myself on the couch, and pondered the clairvoyant's message. Not that there was room for ambiguity.

Between you and me, I think it's all a bunch of hooey, but her eyes! Wide with an authentic terror, I'm certain she lacked the talent to fake. She said the signs were irrefutable. "Your time will stop at half-past nine on Tuesday morning. Put your affairs in order." Then she threw back her fee. Never known a charlatan toss away cash.

She'd draped the crystal ball with a blood red velvet cloth and shoved me out of the door as though I was contagious. Can't recall how I got home, but I assume I trudged through the teeming rain because I was drenched to the skin, with that bone-deep chill which settles deep into your soul.

Cruise, my undersized tomcat blessed with an oversized ego, greeted me in his usual urgent fashion, demanding food, then ignored my existence until he wanted more. Whenever I'm "under the weather", as my granny always said, he scrutinises me, and yowls his concern. Not for my well-being, but at the remote possibility that his routine might be disrupted. Heaven forbid dinner might be late!

We've stared at each other a lot this weekend. He senses something is amiss. I should leave a note asking my sister to adopt him, but she's more likely to bundle him into a sack and chuck him in the canal. They share a mutual hatred, and I can't imagine them bonding in grief over my demise.

9:30 Tuesday couldn't be more anodyne.

Monday, the start of the working week, brings dread, a wilting of the weekend spirit. Wednesday is hump day, halfway to happiness. Thursday involves preparation for Funtimes Friday, knock-off-early-and-forget-your-responsibilities-day. Saturday and Sunday provide opportunities for much needed indulgences after a week of slogging at a desk or whatever gruesome torture to which one habitually submits in exchange for a meagre wage.

But Tuesday? Cheap Tuesday? An utterly boring, nothing-ever-happens-day. The day I'm allegedly destined to die.

Too many embarrassing methods to cark it in public. And if my time is up, I don't want to be responsible for taking anyone else with me, so I can't risk travelling to work. Imagine waking up dead and discovering you were responsible for a train derailment!

I called in sick on Monday. Well, sent a text, then switched off my phone. Couldn't face talking to anyone. They'll find out soon enough.

Went into domestic demon mode. My flat hasn't been this clean since I first moved in. Nothing out of place, surfaces polished, windows gleaming, even though I'm keeping the curtains drawn. I've scrubbed the bathroom to showroom level, and the oven is gleaming like new.

She said 9:30, so I'd normally be behind my desk, deleting all the non-urgent emails and counting down to morning tea, but I'm not risking it. Besides, dying at your desk is such a sad cliché.

How does one dress for a date with Death? I dithered about staying in my pjs, but decided to glam up instead. I'd like to be remembered as put together, not as a shambolic mess. Charcoal trousers, a thunder grey top, and full make up. I even blow dried my hair, because, hey, who wants to pass to the other side and spend eternity looking like a scarecrow who's been dragged through a hedge backwards?

Cruise is brushed, fed, and curled beside me, purring his satisfaction. Will he miss me? Or immediately transfer his fickle feline affections to whoever opens a can of tuna?

Grandmother's ticking clock is the only other sound in my pristine apartment. I hope she'll be pleased to see me, or at least not too disappointed at my lack of outrageous success. She had high hopes for me. I thumb away a solitary tear. Crying over missed opportunities is a smidge pointless now, and I don't want to smudge my mascara.

9:29. I realise I'm holding my breath, and force myself to exhale.

Cruise sits up, instantly alert. He leaps onto the bookshelf, Mission Impossible style, to chase a gecko.

Grandmother's clock crashes to the floor; smashed glass, delicate springs, and tiny cogs skitter across the immaculate tiles.

Cruise swaggers back to the warm spot beside me, a gecko tail held proudly in his murderous maw. He drops the writhing appendage on my lap, indifferent to the destruction of the antique clock.

The hands point to 9:30.

The clairvoyant was right. Time stopped.

A Proper Villian

James and his friends sat cross-legged, passing the multi-layered parcel. Each brightly coloured sheet of wrapping ensured no boy cheated. Avid eyes followed the shrinking package, hoping the next stop would expose the loot.

Nanny cut the cheerful party music as the fat kid took possession. James smirked, certain in his cynical ten-year-old heart Nanny schemed on his behalf.

New to the neighbourhood, and enrolled at the same exclusive school, the fat kid had no friends. His respectable banker father and socialite mother were blithely unaware their darling Ben was associating with the offspring of career criminals.

Red-faced with exertion, Ben beamed victoriously as he unwrapped his prize. The smile faded when he revealed a Fitbit.

Nanny herded the children into the dining room, where the table groaned under the weight of fatty, sugary delights. She smiled grimly as she poured red cordial.

The parents trouped in, wine glasses in hand, to congratulate the birthday boy on achieving double figures, a rite of passage they drunkenly thought laudable. James offered politely murmured thanks and accepted sloppy kisses from aunts, uncles, and neighbours, before moving on.

Bank robbers and art thieves, drug dealers and gambling den proprietors: they lavished expensive gifts on him, in a game of oneupmanship. The fully functional miniature Range Rover was the most splendid gift, making the other boys sick with envy, but even more eager to curry favour and beg a ride.

James peered out of the window at his gleaming new toy. Yes, a proper motor for a proper villain-in-training. Just like Dad's, except not bullet-proofed. Hands in pockets, he jingled his illicit haul. Not one of his victims had noticed his light fingers as he'd relieved them of diamond and ruby encrusted gewgaws while they smothered him with fake affection.

"Well, sonny, what do you plan to be when you grow up?"

James recognised the sharply dressed thug. A distant relative who'd made his immense fortune offering spurious protection to vulnerable businesses. His cauliflower ear and scarred jaw repulsed James. *Nothing like you.* "Rich," James said. "Rich and happy."

"Following in the old man's footsteps, eh?"

They glanced at his father and his vigilant minder.

"Yes, Sir. But better. I won't get caught."

"Cocky little fu- fella, ain't ya?" The racketeer drifted back to the throng of adults, disconcerted by James' self possession and wary of giving offence to a future crime-king. A line he wasn't foolish enough to cross.

James studied the group from the corner of his eye: besuited men, massaged and manicured; painted and powdered women, glittery with gold and jewels. The adults fawned and jostled for his father's attention, while unruly, sugar-fuelled boys enforced their fierce hierarchy on Ben, the unlucky outsider.

James pushed through the mob. "Big Ben, fancy a ride later?" Simple words, buying a lifetime of loyalty. James smiled at his first recruit. "I need a new sparring partner."

A wide smile slowly spread across Big Ben's moon face. "I'm a championship boxer. Got a cabinet full of cups and medals to prove it."

Everyone gathered around when Nanny wheeled in the massive cake topped with a pyrotechnic miracle. Guarded by Big Ben, James blew out the candles and endured another profitable round of hugs and kisses.

Father always stressed the importance of planning, starting early, getting a jump on the competition. James knew these were the days to lay the foundations of his future empire. Today, he'd gained a staunch henchman, and successfully practised his chosen profession.

Tomorrow, he'd have to return them with an insincere note of apology, but for now, his pride glowed brighter than the birthday candles as he caressed his filched jewels.

Amateurs

"Thought I'd be packed and gone before you got home. I'm leaving, Jess. You've let yourself go, you're fat. I don't fancy you anymore. Don't call me, I'm with someone else now."

She had stood at the foot of their bed, stony faced, unable to respond. Her whole body had frozen with shock and fear: fear of being abandoned, fear of being unloved, fear of being ugly, fear her friends already knew and were laughing at her. How had she not seen this coming?

When the rattle of his car was no longer audible, she ran to the bathroom and puked up her guts. Three years wasted. Three years of adoring him, waiting for him to pop the question while he was looking for a better prospect. Bastard.

Did her friends already know? They knew all the juicy gossip. Shit! What if he'd hooked up with one of them? He'd gotten along with all her friends and she'd revelled in the fact that all her friends liked him. Shame and confusion swept over her in hot waves, leaving her sweaty and shaking.

After showering and washing her hair, she stood naked before the bathroom mirror, turning slowly, twisting her head to see as much as possible. She sucked in her tummy and stood as tall as she could manage.

"Well, Jess, you're not skinny … but you're not bloody fat, either. Cheeky fucking bastard. Not like he's a Greek bloody god. So." She peered into the mirror. "You gonna curl up and be a victim or you gonna channel your inner goddess? Yeah, that's right, you're gonna put on your best ever show next weekend. No doubt he'll be there with his tart. Show him what he's missing."

· · · ● · ● · · · ·

Emma and Chloe had assured her they knew nothing of Liam's affair. They arranged to meet at the pub for pre-race drinks. Too nervous to wait, Jess had arrived early and started drinking with a bunch of people she vaguely knew. Determined to show everyone she was having a good time, she'd drunk too much, too quickly. Her inhibitions fled. Starving and exercising like a demon all week may have been part of the reason she was in this condition. With very little encouragement, she'd clambered on the bar and given it all she'd got.

Her new heels had raised blisters but she'd ignored them. Slipping in spilled alcohol brought her down. Down from the bar in a tangled heap on the sticky floor. One of the heels snapped clean off her gorgeous new shoes. Overwhelmed by pain and embarrassment, she'd curled up and howled. The manager, who had been more than happy to serve her alcohol a few minutes ago, turfed her out with a stream of imprecations, flinging her broken shoe after her.

Jess limped to sit on a flat-topped rock near the front of the pub. Lack of food and an excess of booze whirled around in an impromptu dance to which she didn't know the steps. She lurched into the gardens and emptied her stomach.

The pub was on a slight rise and the views would have been spectacular, marred only by the overflowing car park, had she not been too drunk to focus.

All she'd wanted was to have a good time. Why was that too much to ask? Jess crawled back to the solidity of the rock. A safe place to await her friends. The midday sun was merciless, beating on her head like a brass drum. The pain reverberated with ecstatic abandon. Jess curled into a ball, trying to make herself a smaller target for the searing sunbeams.

The shade was both unexpected and welcome. Holding a hand above her eyes, she peered at the silhouette offering protection from the nuclear orb above.

"Hi, I saw you in the bar earlier. You okay? Thought you might need some water." A bottle, beaded with condensation, was presented.

"Thanks … you're … very kind …" Jess chugged back most of the bottle. "Whoa! I needed that. Do I know you?" She frowned at the tall shadow.

"Nah, I just saw a beautiful damsel in distress, thought I could assist. Call me Jake." He sat next to Jess, who scooted over to make room. "Just here for the races, how 'bout you?"

Jess licked her lips and swallowed nervously. "Local. I'm supposed to be meeting friends from work …" She drank again, partly because she was thirsty and partly to hide her face. Jake's stare was intense, and she realised what a fright she must look: from her blistered feet and broken shoes, to her bedraggled updo. She tentatively touched the loosened fascinator, hanging by a few hairpins.

"Here, let me …" Jake leant in and gently removed the frothy confection of feathers and lace. "Better?"

"I don't feel well." Jess's world was spinning, a kaleidoscope of colour, bright in the centre and dark around the edges. She splayed her hands on the rock to steady herself. "I really don't … I think …"

"You're probably dehydrated, you drank quite a bit, earlier. Here." Jake supported her with one arm while holding a bottle to her lips with the other. "Drink up."

"I can hold it myself," she slurred. Gripping the bottle with both hands to prevent it escaping, she gulped the cool water. Unable to remain upright, she slumped against Jake, horribly conscious of the firmness of his chest and abs. Sculptured, like a statue, a work of art, unreal … Jess involuntarily closed her eyes.

· · · ● · ● · · · ·

Emma and Chloe scoured the bar, searching for Jess.

"Maybe she changed her mind, couldn't face the possibility of running into Liam the Louse," said Emma.

"Check for messages," said Chloe. "If she changed her mind, she'd let us know."

Both flicked through their phones. Nothing.

"I'm gonna call her," said Emma. "She's not exactly herself. She could've … well, let's see where she is." Emma speed dialled Jess's number. "Bloody Hell, can't hear a thing with this racket."

Chloe followed Emma outside and mooched about while Emma tried again.

"Emma! Over here, Emma." Chloe nudged the crushed feathers with her toe. An empty water bottle next to it rolled gently in the breeze. "Isn't this Jess's fascinator?" She looked wide eyed at Emma.

Emma crouched down, frowning in concentration. "You got a plastic bag tucked away, Chloe?"

"What? Yes, why?" Chloe rummaged deep in her bag and produced a neatly folded bag, secured with a rubber band. "What're you doing?" She watched Emma use the bag as a glove, picking up the discarded bottle and top, screwing them together, and wrapping them carefully in the bag.

"Can you see anything else?"

"Such as? What're we looking for?"

"I've no idea, just look around while I call Jess, again. Maybe she's had an accident or something …" Emma pressed the phone to her ear, trying to block out other noises.

Chloe spun in slow circles, then whirled back to look at the car park. She grabbed Emma by the shoulder, spinning her around. "There," she hissed. "Isn't that Jess? With some man? Carrying her? What the fuck?"

Both women chased after their friend, panting and yelling.

"Hey! You, hey you. Stop. Put her down. Hey!" Unencumbered, they caught up and dodged around to block the stranger's path.

"Jess? Jess? Can you hear me?" Emma patted Jess's cheek. "What the hell have you done to her? Fucking pervert!" Emma elbowed her way under Jess's shoulder and took her weight. "Help me, Chloe; get under the other side."

Jake stepped back, raising his hands in the universal signal of surrender. "Calm down, ladies." He smiled, "No harm done, eh?"

"No harm? She's fucking unconscious!" Emma screamed, "What were you planning to do?"

"Look at her foot, it's all black," said Chloe.

"Yeah, that's it, she fell, and I was taking her to the hospital." The stranger grinned.

"And I'm the Easter fucking Bunny," said Emma. "Why didn't you call an ambulance?"

Jess mumbled and drooled, head lolling uncontrollably.

"We've got to get her to the hospital," said Chloe. She fumbled single-handed with her phone, holding it high to get a signal

The stranger retreated, taking keys from his pants pocket. He slid into a Ute two cars away; the engine rumbled to life. "Keep your drunken slut of a friend. I wouldn't waste my time with skanky bitches like you!" The stranger flipped the bird as he roared away.

"What a bastard. Are the ambos coming?" Emma readjusted Jess on her shoulder.

"I was filming him. Look, a great shot of his face, and see …? His registration shows clearly when he pulls away. If he drugged her, and I think he did, we've got him. That's why you collected the bottle, right?"

An Impurrfect Life

I yowl at the offending empty can and turn imploring eyes to Mum. When it comes to pleading, Shrek's Puss-in-Boots is a mere gifted amateur. Me? I'm a pro. A master manipulator. Utterly irresistible.

Mum and I stare into the tuna can void, willing it to magically replenish. I bat it with a paw. Why is my every whim not being fulfilled? With hope cruelly crushed, I shove my nose in and rasp my tongue around the crevices for the phantom fleshy flakes, the tantalising odour making me drool.

Until recently, I had fishy treats on demand; tribute to my feline fabulousness. Now, Dad returns from his hunting expeditions through the echoing supermarket canyons remarkably lightly burdened. He mutters darkly about shortages of canned goods and toilet paper. His failures weigh heavily upon him. Incompetent human. Phttt!

I stretch languorously in a patch of sunlight. Toilet paper, indeed. How ridiculous are humans? I am being rhetorical. That's not a challenge. You don't need to prove your insane ineptitude repeatedly.

Fantasising about fish is futile. Instead, I listen to their furtive conversation. Plebeians wittering on about kindness and community, about sharing, and pulling together — whatever that means.

I watch through sun-slitted eyes as Mum re-checks the larder. None of my tuna, but I spy canned salmon. Hmmm. I twitch my tail in anticipation. Worth a try, even with creatures as unintelligent as humans. Perhaps I can induce her to share.

She returns empty-handed to the couch.

"Watch this," I purr, sitting directly in front of her, and gracefully raising a rear leg over my shoulder. "This is how a superior being avoids toilet paper problems." I demonstrate, slowly and methodically, but realise even if she was smart enough to understand the lesson—which she isn't—she lacks the requisite flexibility to perform gymnastic ablutions.

Mum giggles moronically. "They don't teach that in my yoga class, but I'd like to be that limber."

Dad raises an eyebrow, but wisely says nothing.

Resigned to a fish-free pandemic, I maintain eye-contact as I nudge a mug off the coffee-table to remind her I'm still the boss.

Previously published: Atlas & Alice

May 2020

Chosen Genre

The grubby backpack with the broken shoulder strap remained unclaimed, shoved between two unoccupied seats. I looked around the almost empty train; I was the final passenger. As my stop approached, curiosity overcame me.

The backpack was empty except for a bundle of twelve letters.

Perhaps there would be a clue to the owner's identity inside the letters. If not, I'd drop the backpack at the Lost & Found on Monday. I wasn't stealing; I was sleuthing. Finding its owner would be a game to help pass the lonely weekend.

Fortified by a microwaved meal for one, I dived into my investigations.

The recipient was nameless, cited as Darling or Beloved. The writer described the anguish of separation from his heart's desire and promised to be at the bookshop every Saturday afternoon, forever. Guaranteeing fulfilment of all promises, he signed himself Cowboy.

My track record with romance was limited, and I fantasied all Friday night about a lovestruck buckaroo; a Sam Elliot lookalike, pining for a lover who had ruthlessly abandoned him for an older and wealthier, pot-bellied rancher.

Turning out my wardrobe, I discarded my usual beige attire, in favour of a red silk shirt. With black bootcut jeans and heeled boots, I felt like a new woman. Maybe my cowboy would, too. I smiled hopefully to myself.

· · ● ● · ● · · · ·

Strutting into the bookstore at high noon, I spied him browsing the men's action/thriller section. The black Stetson and string necktie confirmed his identity.

"Howdy, M'am," Cowboy tipped his hat. "Wasn't sure you'd make it." He smiled. "This way."

He escorted me through canyons of bookshelves. My perception blurred in each section. Through Romance he grew taller and chiseled; in Travel he assumed exotic qualities and my widening sleeves sprouted colourful floral embroidery. Roaming through the Self-Help section, I felt a surge of confidence and gravitas. We scooted through Horror and Mystery where he flashed me a hideous skeletal grin. Passing Religion & Philosophy I craved to understand the meaning of life; by mutual unspoken agreement, we skirted Sci-Fi and lingered in Fantasy. Our hands caressed the garish book covers, while a permanent breeze lifted my salon lustrous locks, the silk of my shirt sensuously slithered across my cantaloupe breasts. My muscled thighs bulged under my now leather pants; my booted feet firmly planted on the head of a vanquished mythical monster.

· · ● ● · ● · · · ·

I was unaware the bookstore incorporated a café until I caught a whiff of the pungent coffee. My stomach rumbled, louder than the background music. Ignoring digestive indiscretions, we sat at a secluded table to conclude negotiations.

"Ma'am, you've experienced the options. You seemed kinda taken with Fantasy. If you don't mind me sayin', I thought you'd be a Romance girl, but I guess Cupid's not your bag."

"I'd jump into Romance with you … but that's not how you operate, is it?"

"No, Ma'am. I'm kinda cross-genre. Choose one now, or walk away, forever." He slid a blank book across the table and watched me return to my chosen genre.

Revelling in my newfound assurance, I opened the pages and strode into Fantasy …

The Crystal Pen

The shame! Needing rescuing from an eight week old kitten. If the others ever found out, she'd never live it down. Leaf blushed furiously, angry with herself for such carelessness and with him, the writer, for his blatant greed.

"I can't thank you enough, you saved my life." Leaf panted. "I've never been so scared in my life … if you hadn't come along when you did, well … it doesn't bear thinking about. Thank you." She wilted when she saw the gleam in his eyes.

"Exactly how grateful are you?" he asked as he peered through the bars of the antique birdcage. "Like you say, being mauled and torn apart by those needle sharp claws and scalpel like teeth would be a particularly horrible way to die; especially knowing how Fluffy likes to play." He squinted at Leaf, assessing her. "I thought you were some kind of exotic butterfly at first. I think you can do more than say 'thank you'. I reckon you owe me three wishes, y'know? Like in the stories? Or I could just keep you captive … people would pay a small fortune to see a real live faeric." He smirked through the bars as he carried the cage from the patio to the study.

Leaf shook out her wings, checking for damage and distracting him while she considered her options. The kitten hadn't meant any harm, but had pounced unexpectedly, and Leaf had fled to the shelter of the disused birdcage. The writer had scooped up his kitten and snicked the cage door shut. Too late, she'd realised the cage was iron. Her powers were void.

Leaf made her decision when the writer suggested he could keep her in the cage, in lieu of three wishes. *How dare this stinking clod threaten me?*

Leaf mustered a thin smile. "I'll grant you three wishes, but choose carefully. You're familiar with the stories, so you know once the contract is made, it's irrevocable. No backsies." Leaf paused to make sure he understood. "Jon? May I call you Jon? You must confirm you understand; once a wish has been made, you cannot change your mind at a later date. This isn't down to me; it's the Magical Community Association regulations."

Jon nodded and immediately demanded continuing health and wealth. No please or thank you, Leaf noticed. She made him repeat his first two wishes. She smiled widely as he complied. Predictable wishes, not as imaginative as she expected from a writer. Then again, Jon wasn't a very successful writer.

He reluctantly agreed to release Leaf from the cage so she could perform her magic. Leaf squeaked her indignation when Jon reached into the cage and grasped her in his meaty hand. He blinked when she escaped his grip and reappeared, trembling with resentment, on top of the computer screen. To be handled by a mere bumbling mortal. The humiliation.

Still quivering with mortification, Leaf pointed to the mirror.

"Look closely, you should be able to see a difference."

Jon glanced at his reflection and performed a comical double-take. He leaned in for a closer examination. He ran his fingers through his shiny, bouncy hair and traced his fingertips over his now flawless, glowing skin. He pulled gently at his lower eyelids, marvelling at his bright eyes. His niggling aches and pains had disappeared. He couldn't remember ever feeling this good, thrumming with energy.

"Wow! I look fantastic," he said.

Huh, like a well-groomed bear. A thank you would be polite, you hulking great beast. "You look extremely handsome and fit," said Leaf. "Now, crank up your computer or whatever you do and check your bank balance. Penn & Booker Investments, right?"

Jon's fingers flew over the keyboard as he logged into his bank account. Slack-jawed, he hit refresh. Again and again. Each time the screen refreshed, his balance scrolled higher. Jon leapt from his seat and danced around the room.

"I'm rich, I'm rich. Rich, rich, rich!"

Leaf flitted out of the way when Jon tried to grab her again.

"Don't touch me." Leaf narrowed her eyes. "I'm not your prisoner, nor your pet. A little respect, thanks. I've given my word. If I planned to renege on my promise, I'd already have gone."

Jon nodded grudgingly. He flopped into a chair, chewing his lip as he thought about his third and final wish. Leaf sat atop the mirror and waited, certain he would ask for something foolishly selfish.

With guaranteed health and wealth, what was his heart's desire? He'd spent his entire life writing; unsuccessfully submitting and querying, receiving rejection after rejection, or even worse: no response whatsoever. How bewitching to constantly produce writing which merited awards and for which filmmakers outbid each other for movie rights. Jon nodded slowly. Yes. The perfect wish for any writer. He would be the envy of the writing community.

"I've decided." Jon looked up at Leaf, eyes simmering with greed. "I want to pick up a pen and constantly write acclaim worthy novels. No more writer's block."

Leaf listened carefully to Jon's wish, reminding him once more to consider carefully because there would be no further opportunity to revise his wish, but he was adamant.

"What you're asking requires a lot of effort. I'll need a full day to harness that amount of magic. Crafting the perfect tool takes time."

"Sure, whatever." Jon waved a hand dismissively, already distracted with the refresh button. There were plenty of ways to amuse himself while Leaf created his magic pen. Nothing was out of his financial reach. He planned to have some fun.

Leaf worked slowly and deliberately. Creating an object larger than herself took an enormous amount of energy, but Leaf's motivation burned furnace hot. Not only had Jon the temerity to trap her, but he'd dared to lay hands on her. She shuddered her revulsion. To top it all, he'd dismissed her with a wave of his hand. Not so much as a murmur of thanks. Ingrate.

The crystal pen barrel was full of rainbows, flashing and dancing even in the evening dusk. The gold nib she etched with powerful glyphs unknown to humans. By any standard, the pen was an object of beauty. Any writer would crave such an artefact, to hold it in their hand, to feel the magic.

Leaf housed the magic pen in a solid faerie-gold case with engraved symbols swirling across its glowing surface. Jon's eyes widened and his jaw dropped when Leaf presented him with the promised pen. The case automatically clicked open to reveal the crystal implement sparkling within.

"Jon, don't pick up the pen until you're ready to write constantly. The magic activates when you hold it."

Ignoring Leaf's warning, Jon snatched the pen.

An unexpected warmth surged through his fingers. The pen felt like a natural extension as it swarmed across the creamy white pages, spewing sentence after effortless sentence. Jon was ecstatic. He didn't notice Leaf leave.

He wrote throughout the night, barely able to turn the notebook pages quickly enough to keep up with the flow of words. As the sun came up, Jon realised he'd been scribbling for hours. He'd take a brief nap and get back to work.

The pen refused to release him, dragging his now reluctant fingers across the pages, smearing ink as they struggled to release the enchanted tool. Words flooded over the pages, a torrent of creativity that terrified him. He stood, the pen still scrawling. Jon made it to his bed, where the pen continued to scratch across the sheets.

For days, Leaf fretted about the tiny kitten. When she finally succumbed to her worries and visited Jon, she found the kitten next door with a family who loved playing with her. Leaf heaved an enormous sigh of relief as she sprinkled a dash of faerie dust, strengthening the love between the kitten and her adopted family.

Jon looked thin under his new stubble. Leaf guessed he'd given up cooking and shaving. The notebooks had been filled, and Jon's writing covered the walls. He screamed when he spotted Leaf.

"You tricked me. I'm supposed to be writing bestseller novels, with Hollywood fighting over movie rights." Jon heaved dry sobs; he had no tears left to soothe his red-rimmed eyes.

"I most certainly did not. I gave you fair warning, told you to consider carefully because you can't change your mind once you confirm the wish. You asked to write constantly. That is precisely what is happening. You asked to produce acclaim worthy novels. Hmmm, let me see …" Leaf flittered around the room, perusing Jon's work. She hovered in front of him. "Your work's improved immensely. You received exactly what you requested."

"No, I was supposed to have bestsellers, I was supposed to have Hollywood fighting over me." He thumped his empty fist on the desk; the teetering stacks of notebooks fell to the floor.

"Vain man. Your wealth will continue to accumulate but you'll not have any joy from it; your good health will keep you alive while your magic pen will write immaculate prose forever. Call yourself a writer? You couldn't even craft your three wishes without drawing harm to yourself. Pity you won't have time to attract an agent or publisher." Leaf clasped her hands over her mouth and widened her eyes. "Ooh! That's what you should have wished for: an editor, an agent, and a publisher."

The Hidden Pea

Bella was undoubtedly the most physically attractive woman the Prince had ever met: skin of porcelain, lips like rose petals, lustrous wavy hair, and the most intensely green eyes into which he'd ever gazed. But, she was not a Princess.

Princesses do not wait tables in rowdy roadside taverns.

She noticed him, too. Or at least, she noticed his fine clothes and cultured voice, his gentlemanly manners, and extensive retinue. Not the usual trade. She took a deep breath and turned on a deliberately thousand-watt smile.

The Prince was enchanted, completely captivated. Somewhere, at the back of his mind, he knew his Mother, the Queen, would never approve, but he had lost all sense of reality, helplessly drowning in her charms. He had fallen in love, quite inexplicably, with a common tavern wench. Mother would be horrified.

Mother must never know.

In the last year he'd suffered a perpetual parade of perfectly polished and primped Princesses, panting to be his partner. All were educated, talented, beautiful, and variously skilful. The Queen found fault with each one. Only the most perfect Princess would do for her son. She found each less perfect than the last: one had coarse hair, one oily skin; one spoke too quietly, one too loudly; one was too deferential, one too outspoken; too thin, too plump; too short, too tall; over or under educated in the arts or the sciences. The Queen rejected them all while the virgin Prince had been willing to love which ever one won her Royal approval.

Bella was different. She was perfection personified. Except for the pesky part of not being a Princess.

Over a period of months, the Prince contrived to see her on many occasions, each time becoming more deeply besotted.

His fine manners, beautiful clothes, and sophisticated speech impressed Bella. She considered that this mystery man might make an excellent husband. Just like her favourite dessert, he was rich and thick. Then, he let slip his true identity. Shocked beyond speech, Bella fled. The Queen was infamous throughout the land for her extreme possessiveness and her interference in the Prince's life. Bella was fully aware the Queen would not only reject her, but would most likely find some means to punish her. Bella hid away to consider her options. This was a huge potential prize if she handled herself well. The graft would require precise planning and exquisite execution. But she was an ambitious girl.

As a good Prince in love should, he sought Bella assiduously. After several weeks, Bella arranged for the Prince to find her. He swept her into his arms, crushing her to his velvet clad chest and declared his undying passion.

Feigning decorum, Bella regretfully but firmly pushed him away, tearfully explaining she understood they could never be together, that the Queen would never approve their unequal union. Although she loved him beyond all measure, she insisted they must part. Forever. Her life would not be worth living now, with her one true love denied to her by a cruel fate.

As expected, the infatuated Prince made of all kinds of rash promises he did not know how to keep.

Over several languorous afternoons, Bella extracted as much information about the Queen as she could. She learned in detail all the "faults" of the rejected Princesses. A shadowy idea began to form in the dark recesses of her mind. Bella took some time to flesh out a plan before sharing it with the enraptured Prince. By the time she was finished, the Prince was immensely proud of "his" plan and thought himself an awfully clever fellow. He begged Bella to participate. With cast down eyes, she humbly agreed.

The Prince assumed a hermit-like existence, eating and drinking little, and staying indoors. He neither hunted nor danced, he eschewed cards and avoided his friends. He grew thin and pale. The Queen was quite distraught and begged him to resume his previously lively character. He regretfully explained to his Royal Mother that, having met every available bachelorette and finding them unsuitable, he resigned himself to a life of solitude and contemplation. Obviously, no woman could ever match his Mother's pinnacle of perfection and he couldn't allow himself to settle for second best.

This announcement stunned the Queen. She had never considered that her son wouldn't marry. He had a duty to continue the dynasty. She wanted grandchildren. Perhaps she had been overzealous in her search for the perfect Princess.

With renewed fervour, she sent out a flurry of invitations to every possible prospective Princess, inviting them to an unprecedentedly lavish formal ball. Each Royal Lady returned an apology. Some regretfully declined because they were washing their tower-length hair on the night of the ball, others planned to have a headache. Some had already snagged husbands and were globetrotting on honeymoon ... the excuses were endless; not one acceptance. Even imperfectly proportioned and unpolished

Princesses have a pinch of pride to protect them from possibly perfidious proposals.

The Queen and the Prince fell into an uneasy rhythm. Following Bella's instructions, he continued his new hermit-like existence, seeing his Mother just frequently enough to keep her permanently alarmed about his wellbeing.

One dark, wet, and miserable afternoon, the castle received an unexpected visitor. The servants had tried to shoo the bedraggled baggage to the back door, but she had firmly and politely insisted she was a Princess under the curse of a wicked wizard.

The Queen heard the kerfuffle and intervened, partly through boredom and partly—well, actually, completely through boredom. She sent orders for the servants to treat the storm-drenched wench as though she was in fact a genuine Princess. She ordered hot baths drawn, and beautiful clothes and costly cosmetics supplied. The young woman, when presented to the Queen, made a surprisingly good first impression.

The gorgeous girl revealed how a wicked wizard had cursed her because she'd refused his amorous advances. Her father's distant kingdom declined, crops failed, and the wizard condemned her to wander until she found True Love. The Queen noted the musicality of her voice, the elegance of carriage, and the modest demeanour of the young woman. She looked and sounded like the perfect Princess.

Rather than relegating her to the kitchen to sup with the servants as originally planned, the Queen invited Bella to dine with her Royal self and her beloved son. Bella accepted graciously as a Princess should.

Throughout dinner, the Queen paid careful attention. Bella was exquisite, utterly perfect. Her manners, her voice, her demeanour. Just perfect. But the Queen had one final test.

A host of ladies-in-waiting, who were under strict instructions, escorted Bella to her chambers. After helping her disrobe and dress for bed in a lace-frothed nightgown, they led Bella to her bedchamber, with a bed stacked almost ceiling high with super soft mattresses. Bella climbed the ladder and laid herself down.

All night the ladies-in-waiting sat up, listening to Bella toss and turn, trying unsuccessfully to find a comfortable position. By morning, everyone was thoroughly exhausted.

Even after a sleepless night, Bella was radiantly beautiful. The Queen carefully questioned the ladies-in-waiting, who all confirmed how Bella tossed and turned all night but not once complained.

When the Queen asked Bella if she had slept well, Bella apologetically confessed she had not. In fact, the bed was so lumpy she'd hadn't slept a wink.

Satisfied at last, the Queen kissed Bella. Now she was sure of her Royal heritage, she insisted Bella stay with them and become better acquainted with the Prince.

Much to the Queen's delight, the Prince regained his former vigour. Bella insinuated herself into the Queen's confidence and became an almost constant companion, sewing, reading, or making music together. If she wasn't with the Queen, she was with the Prince. They didn't sew or read together, but they did make … music.

They laughed together at how well their plan was working. If the Queen hadn't overplayed her hand with the ridiculous mountain of mattresses, Bella might not have worked out the ultimate test.

Within a few months, the Queen announced her intention that the Prince should marry Bella, which delighted both young people.

All the previously rejected Princesses attended the wedding. Curiosity overcame jealousy. Who was the mysterious paragon who had inveigled her way into the querulous Queen's good graces? Not one of the perplexed Princesses could recall seeing Bella at any other Royal gathering. Of course, that was neatly explained by the wicked wizard's curse.

Bella consolidated her position by immediately becoming pregnant. This news delighted everyone, naturally.

Bella was almost content in her new role. Until she considered the Queen's relative youth and how much influence she still exerted over the newly wed Prince. Bella couldn't help but notice how the Queen always dressed in long and excessively elaborate skirts and how treacherously steep were the many castle staircases. It was something on which she pondered until a shadowy plan emerged from the dark recesses of her mendacious mind.

Hansel & Gretel: The Verdict

The Woodcutter had caught Hansel and Gretel red-handed at the scene of the crime. Drifting smoke and fleeing wildlife had alerted him that something was frighteningly wrong in the forest.

After weeks of legal preparation, he gave evidence. Hobbling on crutches, he explained to the court how he'd burst into the glade where the Sweet Old Lady lived in her traditional gingerbread cottage. "I ran as fast as I could, but the cottage was already afire. The accused pair of awful adolescents were dancing maniacally around the blaze, stuffing themselves on stolen candy. I suspect they were acting under the influence of ice-ing, Your Honour."

A shocked murmur rippled around the courtroom.

Prompted by The Tin Soldier acting for the prosecution, the Woodcutter tearfully continued. "They pretended they'd just arrived and claimed to be searching for a way in to rescue the Sweet Old Lady, but the remnants of their stolen picnic told a different story. They had even toasted marshmallows while callously ignoring her screams for help."

"Is it true," The Tin Soldier asked, "that at great risk to yourself, you braved the fierce flames, broke through the confectionery walls, which were collapsing and dripping molten sugar into a lava-hot lake of syrup, and found the Sweet Old Lady trapped under a chocolate log?"

The Woodsman wiped a tear and nodded.

"I put it to you, ladies and gentle creatures of the forest, that with multiple fractures, severe burns, and inhalation of scorched sucrose, the unconscious Sweet Old Lady would have certainly died without the Woodsman's selfless actions."

The Three Little Pigs took their places in the witness box. "We organised a water bucket chain," the first pig said.

"We couldn't save the gingerbread house from ruin, but we prevented the fire spreading throughout the forest," the second pig said.

"We saved the bacon of many grateful residents," the third pig said.

Snow White provided a character witness statement. "The Sweet Old Lady taught me to cook when I got the housekeeping position with the Seven Dwarves. She regularly dropped off elaborate confections for the boys, in exchange for help with odd jobs around the cottage she could no longer manage in her frail old age."

Next, The Three Bears testified to her generosity. "She gives us honey from her beehives for our porridge, in exchange for baskets of fresh forest fruits."

The Three Blind Mice praised her hospitality for allowing them free run of her home in return for keeping down the insects attracted by the sugar. "Our disability makes us particularly vulnerable in the forest," they said in unison. "We're currently staying at an Airbnb with The Old Lady Who Lived in a Shoe. Not an ideal situation, what with all the kids running around."

The court suspected the awful adolescents of being part of a housebreaking gang, headed by a female known as "Goldilocks", but there was no substantive proof and these two tough teens remained tight-lipped during their remand period.

Meanwhile, the Woodland folk formed a committee to re-build the Sweet Old Lady's house. Snow White whipped up commercial sized blocks of confectionery. A local dragon kept the ovens running twenty-four seven. The Three Little Pigs used their building experience to design a modern single-storey cottage. The Sweet Old Lady hoped to be mobile with the aide of striped candy canes, but needed wheelchair access included, just in case. The Three Bears and the Seven Dwarves provided most of the labour and organised the teams of volunteer villagers. Mr Wolf provided site security. An unspecified number of his pups enlisted to guard the Sweet Old Lady and her new cottage indefinitely. Rumours of reprisals by the Goldilocks' gang were rife and outraged the community.

Mr B B Wolf escorted handcuffed Hansel and Gretel from the holding cells to the dock to hear the court's verdict. His bared teeth and raised hackles prompted their reluctant compliance. "Grrr." A throaty growl escaped from between his gleaming canines. Judge Miller glared at the unrepentant perps. They stood with heads up, defiant and proud, showing no remorse for their heinous crime.

Judge Miller wore a solemn expression as he handed down his verdict. "Because the Woodcutter acted promptly, the Sweet Old Lady will recover, although her stay in hospital will be long and her physiotherapy longer. I find the accused, Hansel and Gretel, guilty of attempted murder, arson, deprivation of liberty and a handful of minor property related offences. Coming from a broken home and not having positive role models is not an excuse for such egregious behaviour."

Hansel surged to his feet. "Your Honour, the Sweet Old Lady couldn't possibly eat all those toothsome goodies. We were hungry orphans, and she's a selfish old witch. Any decent person would have invited us to eat our fill."

The juvenile gangster, Gretel, jumped to her feet and joined the tirade. "If she'd just let us help ourselves, we wouldn't have needed to lock her in. It's her own fault for not sharing."

The jury gasped as the self-entitled young miscreants destroyed any remaining sympathy. Their complete lack of remorse demonstrated their unfitness for rehabilitation.

Judge Miller rapped his gavel. "For your own safety, I sentence you to be pricked with an enchanted spindle, which will induce a magical coma. You will remain in the tallest tower of the abandoned castle until someone is foolish enough to kiss you both awake."

Aided by Jack the Giant Killer, The Woodcutter planted a hedge of quick growing thorns around the dilapidated castle. He wiped his calloused hands and muttered, "If that pair thinks a handsome prince will wake them up with a kiss in a hundred years, they're living in a Fairytale."

Social Climbing

Cutpurse Jack's hand closed around the rough speckled egg. A shattered skull peered from the nest of rocks, branches, and snapped femurs. His mouth dry with fear, Jack placed the treasure into a padded pouch and secreted the pouch inside his tunic. Above, the gigantic fire-birds wheeled in the cloudless dawn skies as they searched for prey.

Thieving came as naturally as breathing to Jack. Wallets and pocket watches, gold chains and brooches were his usual fare, items easily converted into small coins in seedy venues, located down dark unnamed alleys. But stealing the last egg of the final pair of fire-birds was his most audacious and dangerous heist, an open challenge with potentially life-changing results.

If he survived.

Over the last year, Jack had grown thin, but his stash had grown fat. Enough to pay the mage for a glamour and an invisibility spell.

"Because there's less of you," the wizard had said, "the invisibility spell will last longer. Only a few minutes more, but a lot can happen in a few minutes."

Vicious winds whipped at Jack on the pinnacle of the mountain and he squeezed shut his eyes. He slithered and slipped from the nest and skittered down the scree. The invisibility spell still worked, only the cascades of pebbles betrayed his presence. Jack crawled on all fours to the spurious safety of the collar of rocks encircling the neck of the mountain. The fire-birds swooped closer, but spied nothing to interest them.

Jack caught his breath and checked the contents of the pouch. Still intact. He dodged between house-sized boulders and startled a herd of shaggy mountain goats, who scattered when they scented his nervous sweat. The circling fire-birds screamed and dived, performing impossible acrobatic feats to turn talons first to their elusive prey. Bleating and blatting, the goats leapt from rock to rock, defying death and gravity with the same panache as Jack defied guard patrols and locked doors.

Jack's silhouetted shadow warned him the spell was fading. While the goats distracted the birds, he scuttled further down the mountain and darted into the leafy undergrowth, where his shadow mingled with older and colder shades. Dappled sunlight painted a false reality and Jack stepped carefully over the moul-dering leaf litter, alert for rabbit traps or worse. The guardians of the fire-birds were reputed to set man traps and leave the wolves and bears to finish the remains.

The pulsating heat from the egg warmed his chest, both reassurance and threat.

Twin screeches of fury alerted Jack the fire-birds had discov-ered their loss. He didn't hang around to watch them hunt the culprit.

Jack hacked a thin sapling and stripped away its fresh limbs and leaves. He poked the ground before stepping forward. A slow and tedious method of traversing the forest, but recommended if you intended to reach the far side in one piece.

The midmorning sun warmed Jack's face as he emerged from the forest and skirted the edge of a tidy fishing village. A swollen river wended its serene way to the capital. The few boats up-turned on the shoreline were neatly arranged like young scholars waiting to be called upon to repeat their lessons. Jack took his time. As far as he could tell, the menfolk were fishing, and the womenfolk were tending their hearths. Chickens scratched in the dirt and pigs rooted for worms and insects on the riverbank. Neither group paid him any attention.

As stealthily as a shadow, Jack slid a small rowing boat into the shallows. Staying low, he allowed the craft to float into the middle of the river, where the stronger, faster currents seized hold and hurled him downstream. Once clear of the village, Jack sat up and grabbed the oars. He rowed with a metronomic rhythm.

Fat cows nodded in lush water meadows, and lambs gambolled in close-cropped fields. The sun crept to its zenith and still Jack rowed, adding his youthful puny strength to the ancient force of the flood-fed river.

As the afternoon shadows lengthened, the turrets of the capital city loomed on the horizon, and Jack scanned the bank for a suitable landing place. Getting caught in the rapids which raged around the city's weirs would attract too much of the wrong attention for even a man of his considerable expertise.

Jack steered his stolen boat into the shallows on a shaded bend and tied the craft to a drooping willow, which doubtless grieved for his lost honesty. He sloshed through calf deep water and eyed the surrounding fields. Bovines and equines were the only witnesses to his unusual arrival. The cows lowed and continued to graze. The horses flicked their tails, all except one, a nag of no particular distinction other than nosy. Jack pulled a coil of rope from one of his many pockets and approached the mare. He crooned nonsense as he fashioned a bridle and led her to a tree stump.

"Would you like to see the city, my curious friend?"

The mare whinnied and pricked her ears, pleased to receive attention. She nudged Jack's pockets, her dark eyes filled with hope.

"Oho, nothing there, sweet girl, but I'll find you something when we get where we're going." He patted his chest to reassure himself the egg still nestled in its pouch. Jack straddled the horse, who calmly carried him through the gate and onto the rutted track. Jack laid low across her withers until certain he was past hailing distance of her rightful owners, then sat up and kicked the mare into a bone-jarring canter.

Thrushes and blackbirds carolled unbridled joy at spring's abundance and Jack whistled merrily but tunelessly in celebration of his anticipated riches.

The grey city walls grew taller the closer he rode. Colourful pennants snapped in the stiff breeze, polished helmets gleamed, and spear tips glittered in the bright sunlight. Country folk trundled wheelbarrows of parsnips and lettuce, more affluent traders guided horse or oxen drawn carts, while men in breastplates and greaves astride proud prancing horses jangled through the gates. The sentries nodded threadbare Jack and his nondescript nag through without a second glance.

"I promised you a treat," Jack said. "I'm a man of my word." He slid to the cobbles and lead his mount through the teeming markets. By the time he'd reached the other side, his pockets bulged with apples, pears, and carrots swiped from unsuspecting stall holders. Jack led his nag down a dingy street and offered the illicit goodies. They disappeared within her velvety maw almost as quickly as Jack had purloined them. She lifted her tail and dropped a steaming hot thank-you for anyone with a shovel.

Once again, Jack patted his chest; once again reassured by the hot bulge nestled above his heart. He rummaged through his pockets and produced two packets of waxed paper. The larger packet he opened first and offered the contents to the nondescript nag. She licked the paper clean with one slobbery swipe of her tongue. The air shimmered around her and her coat shone, her hooves gleamed and her reins jingled with silver bells. She arched her muscled neck and shook her full mane.

Jack tore open the second, smaller packet and swallowed the contents. Fur trimmed velvets replaced his faded and patched clothing, and soft as butter leather boots encased his feet. A feathered hat perched atop his head and lent him a rakish air. Rings twinkled on his fingers.

He leapt astride his horse, and they trotted through the town, admired by all who saw them. He arrived outside the castle gates as the sun kissed the horizon, making the sky blush a furious crimson.

"The King will wish to see me," Jack called to the guards. "I have brought the last egg of the fire-birds."

The Captain sent messengers to the King, while he detained Jack in an outer room.

"This is the last day of the contest," the Captain said. "Seasoned warriors and hardened soldiers set out in high hopes, but none have returned."

"I saw their remains," Jack said. "Brave men."

The Captain looked for weapons and armour, but saw only what appeared to be a soft-palmed wealthy merchant. "It doesn't count if you purchased the egg. You must have climbed the mountain yourself."

"But of course." Jack winked. "I never pay for something which is there for the taking."

A page scurried into the room, pink and breathless with excitement. "The king will see you now."

Jack removed his hat and adjusted his unfamiliar garments. "Lead on."

The king sprang from his throne and strode to meet Jack. "You are the final contestant. The sun has set. None others have returned. Show me the egg."

"Does the deal still stand, Your Majesty? You will bestow your daughter upon the man who brings you the last egg of the fire-birds?"

"Yes, yes. The only thing a man really has is his word. Show me the egg."

Jack hesitated. "I'm not sure I want to marry a princess, Your Majesty. We may not find one another pleasing."

The King grew red, and he roared. "My daughter is the most beautiful girl in the kingdom. No other surpasses her beauty or wit. How can she not be pleasing?"

Jack shrugged. "Appearances are not everything, Your Majesty, and I would not marry any girl who did not love me for who I am."

"Show me the fire-bird egg. Then we will discuss terms."

Guards with spears and swords lined the perimeter of the throne room. Jack saw no profit in arguing. He pulled out the pouch and unlaced the neck. He dropped the throbbing egg into the King's cupped hands. The King immediately dropped the egg into a waiting brazier.

A thin screech, sharp as a rapier, cut the air and the egg shell shattered. A fist sized ruby glowed in the embers, and dark indistinct shapes swirled within. The stone swelled and throbbed in the heat as the embryonic fire-birds grew.

From behind a marble pillar stepped a beautiful woman. "Father? Is this my husband?"

Jack dropped to one knee, head bowed.

"The foolish fellow wants to renegotiate," the King said. "He wants to marry a woman who loves him."

Jack coughed. "A woman is not a horse to be bought and sold, nor led astray by soft words, Your Majesty."

"Who are you?" the Princess asked. "Other men compete for my hand, yet you shy away. Why are you different?"

Jack looked up at the Princess as she frowned upon him. "Princess, do you not wish to marry a man you at least like? I cannot, in conscience, marry a woman I won as a prize."

The Princess tapped her foot. "Without doubt, you are brave. You climbed the mountain and stole the last fire-bird egg, yet I see neither armour nor weapons. You bear no family crest and I can not categorise your features as belonging to any family. Who are you?"

"I have no pedigree, but I am a man of my word. After all, a man's word is the only thing which cannot be stolen."

So began Jack's journey up the social ladder with a woman whose interest he kindled and whose heart, piece by piece, he stole.

Verity

I landed in a tangle of limbs and bicycle. The bike had fared better than me. The handlebars were skew-whiffed, but nothing else obvious at first glance. I wasn't so lucky. My mouth was bleeding, my arms and legs were oozing blood from multiple cuts and grazes, and my left pinkie finger was bent at an awkward shape and was a funny colour. I heard the loud hiccupping sobs before I realised they were mine. I tried to stifle them, but it was too late.

The witch was coming for me! There was no escape!

She stood over me, assessing me, head cocked to one side as she calculated if she could squeeze me into her oven. I crab walked backwards, untangling myself from the frame of my bike and scrambled to my feet. Quick as a snake, she grabbed my wrist, pulling me close and peering at my left hand.

"Not too bad, dislocated but not broken." She smiled. "Come."

Still holding my wrist, she picked up my bike with her other hand and walked towards the front door. Too terrified to scream, I stumbled along next to her.

Every neighbourhood kid knew about the witch. Glimpses of her were rare and nobody had ever seen her up close, let alone spoken with her. We never saw her around the town. She didn't shop at the supermarket. We knew that meant she hunted kids and stray pets. We knew she kept them in cages and fattened them to eat.

Now she had me by the wrist and was dragging me into her lair. I was a skinny kid, so she'd need to keep me prisoner for weeks, maybe months, before I was plump enough for eating. I could refuse to eat, but that would only make me weak and I'd need to be strong to escape. It was a known fact no one had ever rescued a child from this house; the witch was too clever and powerful. I'd need to plan my escape carefully.

Propping the bike next to the door, the witch manoeuvred me through a pastel-painted hallway and into what must have been a kitchen, although it didn't look like any kitchen I'd seen. Then again, I'd not seen a witch's kitchen before.

She guided me to the table.

"Sit." She indicated the chair and pushed me towards it. "Rest your hand here." She shoved a folded tea towel under my hand and smiled at me. "Let's get you cleaned up first."

First! First! Then eat me when I was clean?

She fussed at the sink, returning to the table with a large bowl of warm water with bits of green floating on top. A weird smell rose with the steam, I instinctively pulled back in my chair.

"Relax, this part shouldn't hurt."

This part! So the next part will hurt? Shouldn't! So it might? Relax! Was she serious? No way I was relaxing, I prepared myself to explode into action and make a mad dash for freedom before she caged me and tried to fatten me.

"You're Charlie, right? The Johnson kid? Hello Charlie, we've not been properly introduced. You can call me Verity."

Open-mouthed, I watched as she cleaned my cuts and grazes with a soft cloth which she dipped in the funny smelling water.

So far, it didn't hurt. In fact, the water must have been magical, because the stinging pain faded.

I flinched when she wiped my face.

"Sorry," she apologised. "Here, spit it into this." She was offering a tiny cup, hand painted with pretty flowers. I shook my head. Raising an eyebrow, she looked from me to the cup and back again. Reaching behind her, she grabbed a box of tissues. "Will these do?" Her green eyes crinkled as she smiled.

Nodding, I took one. Without taking my eyes off her, I spat the tooth into the tissue and shoved it into my shorts pocket. Everyone knows you don't let witches have teeth or nail clippings they can use in spells against you.

The witch went back and forth several times, emptying and refilling the bowl. She was very thorough, and the stinging disappeared. Evidence of powerful magic.

"Thank you," I muttered.

She smiled at me again and nodded. "They're just garden herbs. It's not magic. Now, this smells odd, but it will help with the bruising." Opening a jar she'd plucked from many on the shelves lining the walls, she applied a dollop of paste to my shin and another to my arm. "You need to keep this clean, your mom will change the dressing for you. You'll take a jar of this with you."

Mom! Take with me! Maybe she wasn't planning to eat me.

As she wrapped gauze over the grazes, I allowed myself to relax - just a tiny bit. The kitchen walls were covered in shelves packed with jars of all imaginable sizes. A few were empty but most contained bits of plant: leaves, seeds, bark, twigs, and dried flowers. Some had liquid with unidentifiable bits floating in them, others had what looked like the goo mom put on her face to keep away the wrinkles. She called it her "magic cream".

Verity noticed me eyeing the jars. "My natural pharmacy," she said with a nod to the jars. "Whatever aches and pains you've got, I've got a remedy to help you feel better. Old-fashioned stuff I learned from my mom and my granny. Seems to work. How are you feeling? I bet the sting has gone."

I nodded cautiously. "Yes, much better, thank you," I replied, trying to remember my manners.

"Next then. Bathroom's just down the hall. Go on and swish out your mouth. Use this." She offered a wine glass filled with … something. "It'll stop your gum hurting."

I noticed her beautifully manicured hands as I reached for the glass. Not gnarly witch talons. I followed her directions to the bathroom and discovered a wonderland of pale pink and gentle greens. Trying not to make a mess in this delicately lovely room, I swished my mouth, spat in the sink and repeated. The stuff in the wine glass tasted of Christmas. I rinsed the sink before I left.

"My mouth tastes like Christmas," I blurted as soon as I reached the kitchen, knowing as I said it how silly I sounded.

"Cloves. They take away the pain and stop infection. Most people only use them at Christmas in special seasonal recipes, but I've always got them on hand. Very good for toothache." Verity indicated I should resume my seat. There was a glass of milk and a plate of chocolate biscuits waiting.

Verity picked up my hand with the bent pinkie. I repressed a squeal, but it hurt – a lot.

"Hmmm, sorry Charlie, but this bit will hurt. It'll only take a second. Wait until I've done before you have your snack, don't want you to choke. Put your hand back on the table, please."

Not knowing what else to do, I complied. Then I screamed.

Verity had grabbed my hand, and with surprising speed and skill, pulled my finger. She must have known what she was doing, because after a few seconds of agony, it settled to an angry throb. My finger was back in place. I could even wiggle it.

"Thank you very much," I gulped tearfully.

Pushing the box of tissues towards me once again, "Wipe, then eat while I finish." With great delicacy, Verity applied yet more of the paste she'd applied to my grazes. "Comfrey works wonders to help bruising. I'll bandage your two fingers together so you won't wriggle it about while it's healing. Then I'll call your mom."

I gratefully submitted to Verity's ministrations while nibbling the excellent biscuits and sipping the ice-cold milk.

"There! You're all done. Just one thing before I call your mom." Verity whisked out of the kitchen, returning a few moments later, pushing my bike and carrying a toolbox. Without a word, she selected a spanner and set about straightening the handlebars. Stepping back to admire her handy work, she squinted at the chain. Grabbing the bike with both hands, she flipped it over and balanced it on the seat and handlebars. "Loose chain … dangerous," she explained as she tightened it up and expertly flipped the bike upright again.

I was agog with admiration. Not only could she fix people, but she could fix bikes, too! She also baked delicious biscuits!

"That's better." She grinned at me. Verity rapidly punched in a series of numbers while gesticulating that I should eat. "Hi, Mrs Johnson? Verity here … yes, yes, fine thank you … I wanted to let you know Charlie's here with me right now … no, no, fine … she crashed her bike outside my house … no, she's fine now, just a few bumps and bruises … I fixed her up, worst bit was a dislocated finger … no, I don't think so, I've put it back and strapped it, you can take it off in a few days … that's fine, no problem at all. Charlie is a very brave little girl, hardly a whimper

… I think it's tooth-fairy time again … she has it in her pocket … in about half an hour, I expect. She's just finishing up her snack … that would be lovely, I'm looking forward to it … okay then, see you soon."

Verity knew my mom. She knew her number off by heart. They must be friends. Wow!

Just wait until I told everyone. No one would believe Verity had a pretty bathroom and beautiful hands and made awesome cookies.

I beamed my thanks at my new friend.

To Freedom

*D*amned dragons!

Baz burrowed further into the narrow tunnel. He envisioned thousands of tons of rock collapsing; dust filling his lungs and choking him. He broke into a trembling sweat as his agoraphobia spiked to new heights.

Why is golden treasure always guarded by a damned dragon? Why not a more manageable multi-headed puppy or a ferocious tiger kitty? How's an honest crook supposed to make a living?

Baz had been sold to a master thief because he possessed an unusual skill set: he could carry a 3D map in his head, and was small enough to squeeze into unimaginably tiny spaces; phobia be damned.

Derek the dragon inhaled deeply and opened one eye. *Here we go again. Another bungling burglar begging to be barbecued.* He stood and shook himself, coins and egg sized jewels fell from between his glossy scales. He shuffled the treasure to a more comfortable position, his leathery wings sweeping the pile smooth. No one ever wanted to know how difficult it is to sleep on a lumpy heap of metal. Derek sighed, his short fiery breath illuminating the useless riches he was condemned to guard. A fat tear plinked to the ground.

Baz gulped as light flickered at the end of the tunnel. He'd be toast if Derek realised he was here. The earth shook; dirt drifted from widening cracks in the crumbling tunnel walls. Derek was moving.

Breathing heavily, Baz started to back away, but froze when he heard Derek whimpering. *What does a dragon have to cry about?*

Against his better judgment, Baz approached Derek's cavernous lair. "Hello? Are you okay?"

"Go away, little man. I don't want to hurt you."

"What do you want?" Questioning a depressed dragon wasn't the cleverest thing to do, but Baz couldn't bear to leave Derek suffering.

"I want to break free, to fly into the golden blaze of a burnished sunset," Derek sobbed. "What do you want?"

"I want to run an art gallery and make marvellous pictures that enrich people's lives."

"What's stopping you?" Derek asked.

Baz the Burglar blinked at the unexpected question.

"My master, for starters. And lack of funds. What about you?"

"It's too late for me, I've grown too big to escape."

"Can't you blast your way out?"

"I don't know which direction. No point bringing the mountain down on myself."

Baz closed his eyes to consult his inner map.

"That wall's nearest the surface." He pointed to the rear of the cavern.

Derek surveyed his prison one last time and nodded, tail twitching in anticipation.

"Let's do this. Gather what you need and climb aboard, little man."

Baz didn't need a second invitation. He filled his bags with treasure, scrambled onto Derek's shoulders, and wrapped his arms and legs around a handy dorsal spike.

Derek inhaled, stood on his hind legs, extended his wings and blasted a huge gout of fire through the mountainside, terrifying the villagers below.

"Onwards, my friend," Baz cried. "To freedom!"

The Emperor's New Advisor

T he Emperor pointed a bejewelled finger. "Fetch that wretched boy."

Armoured guards wielding wickedly sharp halberds ushered the scruffy lad to the rear of the procession. Their grim faces warned him to still his tongue.

His Majesty suppressed a shiver and picked up the pace, horribly conscious his not-so-white, not-so-tight underwear had seen better days. The entire town gawped and sniggered at his less-than-lovely long johns.

A blushing lady stepped from the crowd and offered to cover the Emperor's embarrassment with her umbrella, but he roughly declined, determined to play out the farce.

Safe within the castle walls, the court was atwitter with rumours and counter rumours. One fact upon which everyone agreed: the traitorous tailor must pay for his prank. The courtiers stormed his workshop, but the wily weaver had absconded with sacks of gold and silver threads, and his exorbitant fee, leaving a detritus of measuring tapes, scissors and pins.

The Emperor fumed as he hastily swaddled himself in multiple layers of satin and brocade, deliberately choosing older, trusted garments. He marched to the throne room, head high, eyes glittering with fury.

"Out! All of you out! Leave the lad on the floor."

Lords and Ladies swished from the chamber, robust brocades and solid silks rustling as they fled the Emperor's ire.

"Why did you say I was naked?"

The boy raised his head from the marble floor and squinted sideways at the red-faced ruler. "Should I have lied, Your Imperial Majesty? Contributed another thread to the mesh of lies?"

"You put me in an awkward position, boy."

The boy sucked his lower lip. "No, Your Imperial Majesty. 'Twern't me got the town gawking as you paraded your pride. 'Twere those balloon faced advisors."

"Balloon faced?" The Emperor snorted. "You dare disparage my friends and counsellors?"

"Sycophants with rocks for brains, Your Imperial Majesty. Cowards, too spineless to speak uncomfortable truths."

The Emperor gestured. "Come here, boy. Sit by my feet."

The youth shuffled to the base of the throne.

"What am I supposed to do with you? If I admit you were right, then I'm admitting the tailor duped me and all my advisors. I can't do that."

"Unless you were conducting an elaborate ruse to discover if your men are trustworthy?"

The conned Emperor rubbed his nose as he considered the lad's cunning suggestion. "Such brutal honesty deserves a reward. I need courageous men by my side. Will you accept the position of Chief Advisor?"

"If you're employing me to give honest opinions, my first advice is to spread the responsibility. Don't put too much power in any one man's hands, not even mine, Sire. Surround yourself with people who won't try to stitch you up, Your Imperial Majesty, or embroider the truth."

"You mean, measure a man by his deeds, not the detailing on his doublet?"

Disengaged

J acob drops to one knee on the antique Aubusson rug and proffers the open box to reveal a mid-green dollar sized stone set in a chunky sterling silver ring. "Marry me."

The butler hovers, alert for the prearranged signal to bring the champagne.

Emily keeps her hands in her lap. Only her perfectly micro-bladed eyebrows move on her Botox-frozen brow. "What's this?"

"A ten carat solitaire. Don't you like it?"

Emily sniffs. "Hardly the engagement ring of my dreams. Looks like something out of a Christmas cracker."

"Try it on. Please?"

Emily curls her fingers and shakes her head. "There's no point. Even if I accept your ridiculous proposal, I wouldn't be caught dead wearing that ugly thing."

"It's a mood ring, darling. With all your treatments and procedures, your true feelings are a riddle, I haven't the faintest inkling what you're thinking."

Emily holds out her hand. "Show me." She snaps shut the box and turns it upside down to read the maker's label. "You bought this at a craft fair? Seriously?" She tosses the casket back at him.

Jacob slides back into his seat and shakes his head at the waiting staff.

"With all your millions, you offer me a tacky mood ring? If this is your idea of a joke, it isn't funny. Or is that all you think I'm worth?"

Jacob sits back in his chair and folds his arms. "I offered marriage. My heart. Everyone said you were a gold-digger, but I didn't believe them."

Emily blinks.

"I'm glad I discovered your true colours." Jacob reaches into his pocket and takes out a small leather box. "I planned to give you this once you said yes." The two carat white diamond blazes in the candlelight.

Emily blanches. "But …"

"Too late." Jacob nods to the granite faced butler. "Please call Miss Emily a cab."

Errol

There was a distinct nip in the air so early in the morning, and Charlie snugged her jacket tighter as she strode towards her classroom.

"Hey, Charlie, can you give me a hand here?"

Ann, the only teacher who was ever earlier than Charlie, was struggling to manoeuvre a rubbish bin that had been left overnight under a dripping tap. "I can't touch it, can you get it out, Charlie?"

Intrigued, Charlie peered into the depths of the black plastic bin. There was about a hands depth of water in the bottom and floating, inert, some kind of rodent. "Poor thing," murmured Charlie. "Let me just … might still be alive … half frozen … this water's bloody cold …"

Ann stepped back to give Charlie better access and to be out of range should the creature still be alive.

The rat was torpid, but Charlie wrapped it in her scarf and gently chafed it until it began to squirm. "It's still alive, we saved him," she exclaimed.

Ann backed off even further. "What are you going to do? I thought it was dead."

"Do?" Charlie shrugged, "I'll warm him up and see how he goes." Rat clasped firmly to her chest, she hurried to her own demountable and let herself in. There were still about ninety minutes before classes begun so she had plenty of time to deal with the rat. Charlie found a scrap of red flannel in the art cupboard and re-wrapped the rodent. She continued to massage him. "Well, Mr Rat, can't keep calling you that, can I," she murmured. "How about Errol? You know, like in like Flynn? You're lucky Ann found you when she did … I don't think you'd have survived much longer."

Errol surveyed Charlie. He'd not yet regained motor control. He was still chilled.

"You know what you need? You need body heat to warm you up slowly. No funny business now, Errol." Charlie tucked the flannel cocooned Errol down the front of her shirt, leaving his eyes and nose peeking out. "Okay there, Errol? Right, stay quiet, please. We're going down to admin, I've got a few things to do and some stuff to collect. No scaring the office ladies, okay?"

Keeping a warm, protective hand over Errol, Charlie trotted over to the administration block.

"What's that?"

"That's disgusting, Charlie, get rid of it,"

"Oooh! You'll get fleas!"

"What if it bites you? You'll get rabies or something …"

So much for being discreetly hidden.

"For goodness' sakes, ladies! He was half drowned and freezing to death. I couldn't ignore someone in distress! He needs help."

The office ladies and a few other teachers shared looks, making it clear that they had neither sympathy for Errol, nor any understanding of Charlie's compassion.

"It's not someone, it's a bloody rat! You should have killed it! Only you'd be daft enough to name it!"

"Don't listen to the nasty humans, Errol. Come on, we'll get some breakfast." They made their way back to Charlie's classroom, with Charlie murmuring endearments all the way.

She pulled her lunch from her bag and broke off part of her sandwich and a piece of banana. A jam jar lid filled with water did service for a drinking bowl.

Carefully unwrapping Errol on her desk, Charlie offered him breakfast. He seemed comfortable sitting in her hand and looked around.

"I guess you trust me, eh? Well, how about you eat something? You've had quite an ordeal, you must be hungry. C'mon Errol, try this, you must get your strength up."

Errol twitched his nose in agreement and clambered off her hand. Table manners abandoned and under the circumstances excused, Errol demolished the sandwich fragment. Charlie pushed the piece of banana closer and Errol sniffed cautiously and started to nibble. It obviously met with approval and quickly disappeared. Charlie offered more sandwich. Errol accepted with alacrity.

When he'd finished breakfast, he took a tentative stroll around Charlie's desk, exploring the piles of exercise books and stationery. He paid particular attention to the pencils before drinking some of the water.

"I wonder …" Charlie poured a dribble of milk into the lid and Errol slurped it enthusiastically.

"Oh Errol, I really do like you, you're so refreshing," laughed Charlie. "I'd love to keep you, but it wouldn't be fair, you should get back to your own home. Promise me you won't jump into anymore water-filled bins, eh?"

Errol appeared quite recovered and relaxed enough to groom himself. Charlie gently stroked his short, silky fur for a few minutes while gathering her resolve.

"Okay, Errol. Time for you to go back. I think you should go before the kids get here and start making a fuss." Scooping him up and back in her shirt front, she stepped onto the veranda. "We're going to the rainforest garden behind the school hall," she explained. "It's quiet there and I think you'll be fine, lots of places to hide and plenty of food. Huh, not too many humans, so you should be safe."

Charlie stepped into the rainforest garden and looked about: heaps of cover, layers of leaf litter, and no doubt hordes of insects and small lizards. She crouched down, glancing about to check they were not being watched, reached inside her shirt and dropped a goodbye kiss onto Errol's head.

"Take care if yourself," she whispered. "Run free and enjoy." As she deposited Errol gently on the ground, the air exploded in a clatter of wing beats! A furious flurry of brown and white, too fast to see detail. Shocked, Charlie fell backwards and landed on her rear.

Errol was gone!

Scorched by an Old Flame

R ob roared into the pub's pothole riddled gravel carpark in a yellow low-slung sporty number, engine rumbling like a grumpy dragon.

"Nice car." *If you like custard slicks trimmed with glittering chrome.*

"Not mine."

"Your brother's?" I remembered they'd shared an enthusiasm for kit cars.

"It's Jane's." He had the grace to blush. "My fiancé's."

I blinked. When I'd rang him—a foolish impulse—I'd asked if he was married "or anything". Doesn't *or anything* cover the entire gamut of relationships?

If he'd been honest, I wouldn't have agreed to a date. I never poach. Besides, if someone cheats on their current squeeze, why would they treat you any better? Especially when they've been engaged for only twenty-four hours!

But, here I am, all dolled up with killer four inch stilettos. You should have seen the assistant's face when I burst through the door at five minutes to closing, asking for the wickedest "shag-me" shoes they had. But that's a story for another day.

"Where does Jane think you are?"

"With Vincent." His puppy dog eyes gleamed with anticipation.

"Let me get this right. You brother is colluding, to deceive your fiancé?" *Scuzzball.*

My silk dress slithered on the cool leather seats. Rob's Paco Rabanne fought a losing battle with the pine scented air freshener. Not much had changed in twelve years. I tossed the fuzzy green tree shape out of the window.

"Take the A56 south." Like a well trained Labrador, he obeyed. We'd dated for six months in high school, more like a lazy habit than true love.

"Jane hates you."

"She's never met me."

"She hates how you treated me."

"If I hadn't set you free, she wouldn't be with you. She ought to be grateful." Or not. Poor beige cardigan wearing Jane.

We ended up barefoot among the sand dunes at Harlech beach, acting like kids. That's when he pulled out the little square packet.

I collapsed laughing, just like the first time he'd pulled the stunt when we were sixteen.

"I've leave Jane, if you'll have me." He lunged for a kiss, and I legged him up. He landed flat on his back and gazed at me like a whipped puppy.

I couldn't resist. I knelt and stuffed a double fistful of sugar fine sand down his shirt. We ended up caked like sugar cookies.

Back at the car, I shook sand into the footwell and finger combed my hair, deliberately leaving curly strands on the backseat. A generous squirt of Chanel for good measure. Subtle? Me? Never!

I insisted on getting fish and chips, knowing they'd stink out Jane's car, which he'd confessed was his engagement gift to her. Ouch! The takeaway receipt I snuck behind the sun visor.

"Can I call you?" Rob asked when we got back to my car.

"I'm sure you'll call me all kinds of things." I slammed my door and drove away without a second glance.

I hope Jane is happy.

No one deserves a lowdown cheating hound.

Fruit Picking

Not a job engineer Sally had ever expected to be assigned, but extreme circumstances demand unusual actions. Before clambering into the huge caterpillar treaded vehicle, she glanced over her shoulder at the ship, lying in a raw gash in the verdant jungle. Only two days since the crash, but already vines snaked over the lower parts of the craft, tangled green veins roping across the smooth underbelly, embracing and claiming the wounded intruder. The colony must make this unnamed, uncharted, but fertile planet their home. At least for now.

She piloted the battery operated truck to the computer designated location. Equipped with a carbon-mesh basket, a knife on a telescopic pole, and a taser, Sally disembarked. Insects with metre-wide wingspans flitted like stained glass angels through the lush vegetation, but the newcomers had encountered no other fauna.

Intoxicating scents from rainbow coloured blooms perfumed the still air. No birdsong; no furtive, scurrying feet. Only the buzz and whirr of gauzy wings marred the silence.

Alone for the first time since the accident, a tsunami of conflicting emotions broke free. Grief for the dead; guilty relief for surviving; fear of the unknown; exhilaration for her potential future. Tears blurred her eyes, she tripped and landed face down beside a bush with mauve triangle shaped foliage and bright orange fist-sized fruits, which glowed in the dense undergrowth.

Sally sniffed. A tantalising whiff, reminiscent of mango and pear, reminded her afresh of her now long dead home. Licking her lips, she reached for the nearest fruit.

The bush shivered and pulled back.

"What the stardust …?" Crouched on her haunches, she slowly extended her hand.

The fruit bush retreated into a vomit inducing miasma of decay.

Sally gagged and pulled her regulation tee shirt up over her face. "Get a grip, girl. Plants don't move. Must be a hallucination brought on by the reek. This could have medicinal value. I need a sample." The sound of a voice, albeit her own, lent her courage. She pushed herself to her feet and seized the blade.

Two impossible things happened simultaneously. A tendril whipped from the uncooperative fruit bush, twined around the knife, and yanked it from her grasp, while a football-sized flying insect dived from the canopy and stole the taser dangling from her utility belt.

Sally whirled to face her aerial assailant, but the thief zoomed back to the protection of the canopy. A rustle from the bush drew her attention. Slack-jawed, Sally stared as the tendril squeezed the knife and poured the resulting pile of glittering fragments at her feet. Metal and plastic shards rained from the canopy as the winged bandit methodically dismantled the taser.

Sally struggled in vain as vines swarmed her legs and encased her. An overpowering scent rendered her unconscious, a kindness from the flora as they planted their seeds in her warm corpse.

Last Chance

"Five," she said. "You get five spins of the wheel of life, five attempts to get it right." She smiled. "Most people manage."

"And those who don't? What happens to them?"

She shrugged. "Meh. They go to Hell, of course."

"You don't seem overly concerned. I mean, shouldn't an angel want to save people from going to Hell?"

"I don't make the rules, Sugar. But, if it makes you feel better, I was one of those who petitioned for multiple attempts. It used to be one strike and you're out. Some people don't hold with reincarnation, but I think everyone should get another chance."

"How many attempts have I made?"

The angel pursed her lips. "I'm not supposed to tell you, but you won't remember this conversation anyway, so I guess it doesn't really matter. You're one of my most troublesome cases." She sighed. "This is your last chance."

"Bugger."

"Bugger, indeed. If you screw up again, I'll be replaced. Demoted. The equivalent of being sent back on the beat or some crappy desk job. Please God, not filing clerk." She shuddered.

"Sheesh. That's kinda harsh."

"Not really, I get five chances, too."

"What if you screw up all five? What happens to you?"

Her wings quivered. "I'd rather not think about it, but I'd get sent downstairs."

"Downstairs? You mean …?"

"Yeah, Hell. They take your wings and replace 'em with horns and a tail. But you get your own pitchfork, though. Handy for the weekend barbecues. Every cloud has a silver lining. Sometimes ya gotta look hard to find it, though." She frowned.

"I'll do my best, I really will. I don't wanna be responsible for us both going to Hell."

"You can't do more than your best. See ya at the end of the ride, Sugar. Good luck."

·····•·•····

"That's an interesting technique you've got there. Why d'ya lie like that?" The apprentice angel wrinkled her nose. "I'm sure I haven't read that in the handbook."

"Think of it as motivation, rather than lies, Toots. They don't ever remember the conversations, but they develop a conscience, a sense of social responsibility. Y'gotta admit, Sweet-cheeks, I've got the lowest return rate. The stats speak for themselves, and this is a results oriented business."

Loaded (& Legless)

Florence glanced at her watch. Almost time to massage Mr Rogers' amputated leg. She'd heard wild stories from the other nurses how the old sailor lost his leg: frost bite while climbing Everest, gangrene from an untreated crocodile bite in Malaysia, a boating accident in the Bahamas. To Florence, he'd sworn he'd rescued a woman from a Great White attack, and lost his leg to the beast and his heart to the lady who briefly became his wife. But she couldn't live with a man who had a prosthetic leg, even though he'd sacrificed the limb to save her life.

Wavelets slapped the oak hull with playful persistence. The sheets creaked and groaned in symphony, lulling Florence into her usual semi somnolence, as she waited for the imperious old coot to summon her so he could spout spurious tales of derring-do from his time-misted youth.

The tinkle of crystal nudged Florence into action. Mr Rogers enjoyed a cigar and a snort of rum while Florence tended his leg, then he insisted she join him for a glass. The heavily embossed bottles of Facundo Paraiso piled up too quickly in the galley, but Mr Rogers insisted he had no intention of trying to extend his life if the effort involved any form of moderation or moral flagellation.

Mr Rogers squinted through his cigar fug. "I've reached a decision," he slurred, lifting his leather eye patch.

"You giving up the grog, eh? About time." Florence massaged lotion into the scarred stump, her expression carefully neutral.

"I've been waiting for the right time, but I've left it too bally late, so I'm giving it to you." He fumbled with his prosthetic and unscrewed a secret compartment. "You dive don't you?" He shook out a tightly furled parchment and slapped it on the bed.

Florence sighed. "Don't tell me. A secret document leading to Montezuma's missing millions? Or the final resting place of the Holy Grail?"

"No need to be snarky, young lady." Rogers stifled a hiccup. "This is a map to the largest treasure trove ever known. King John's royal treasure, presumed lost in a Norfolk swamp, but I know better." Rogers tapped the side of his red-veined nose and winked. "I stole this map from an English lord decades ago, as a student dare."

Florence harrumphed like an irritated hippopotamus.

"The Royal booty wasn't lost; the Frenchies stole it. They were losing the war and one young Duke, with bigger balls than the rest, hijacked the King's train and loaded the gold onto a waiting ship. Poor bugger wasn't much of a sailor. A vicious storm blew him off course and he capsized in the Strait of Dover."

"Let's pretend I believe your preposterous story," Florence said. "Why me?"

Rogers wriggled upright on his pillows. "You're not a nurse. You're an adventurer, like me. I respect that."

"With respect, Mr Rogers, you're full of shit."

He upended his prosthetic and out tumbled a gleaming gold medieval coin. "Wanna bet?"

Not The Girl With The Pearl Earring

I stalk the aisles of overflowing tables twice before I spot her. Grubby and badly framed, a pale-cheeked girl in a tight bodice peers under her lashes.

My accomplice hovers at my elbow, alert to my signals. "What's your best price?" She points to the portrait.

The stallholder checks the ticket. "Says fifty, but today's been slow and I'm about to pack up." He lowers his voice. "Forty for you, my lovely."

She picks up the painting and pretends to examine the frame. "My gran might like this if it was cleaned up. She has terrible taste. Will you take a twenty?"

The vendor rubs his gloved hands. "Thirty-five, and that's my absolute best."

"Nah. I can get something more cheerful at the dollar store." She shakes her head and wanders to the next table.

The trader mutters and replaces the picture. I recognise the paint strokes and the subject. She might not wear a pearl earring in this study, but those melancholic features are unmistakable. I hover at the table, feigning interest in a willow pattern platter. The ticket price is twelve dollars.

The stallholder pastes a smile on his tired face. "I'll give you that for a tenner. Save me packing it up."

I run a finger over the hairline crack. "Wouldn't trust myself to get it home in one piece, mister. Are they the real deal?" I nod at a pair of Georg Jensen salt and pepper shakers.

He brightens as he scents a potential sale. "Mid-twentieth century. Solid silver. Danish classics. These'll never go out of style." He hefts the salt cellar then drops it into my hand. "Quality, my lovely."

"Probably beyond my budget. I'm looking for Christmas gifts for my mum and my ghastly mother-in-law. My mum would love these. She's a big fan of Scandinavian designs." I summon my most winning smile.

"I can tell they'd be going to a good home," he said. "Someone who appreciates class. One fifty, just for you."

"That's a fair price, and Mum would really love them, but that's my entire budget. I still need something for the monster-in-law." I open my purse and count fifteen ten dollar notes. "Would you throw in that tatty picture?"

The man laughed. "You don't like your mother-in-law?"

I shrug. "She's alright. A bit pretentious and old-fashioned. She likes that kind of twee stuff."

He glances at his watch and sighs. "Just for you, my lovely."

My greatest vice, and my special skill, is seeking hidden bargains. The silverware was an excellent find, but the Vermeer was a steal.

Ocean Predators

"Tell me again."

Thom stabbed the navigation chart with his diver's knife. "All you have to do is sprinkle a little party powder where he'll see you. The old fool won't be able to resist and he'll try to score. Act reluctant at first. He doesn't know how to take no for an answer. Make sure he gets the bag I marked."

Angela frowned. "You want me to get him stoned, then invite him on a midnight dive? What if he says no?"

Thom rolled his baby blues. "Use the assets I paid for. Six-inch heels and a string bikini; he won't refuse. We'll clean him out, and split the proceeds, just like always, babe."

Angela nodded. Billionaire playboy, and now recluse, Randy Rex was their most ambitious mark. With a handful of successful operations behind them, Angela and Thom had bulging offshore numbered accounts, cleverly hidden under a multiple shell companies. *Bait. That's all I am to Thom. Without me, he'd be nothing. I don't need him. The meathead only drags me down.*

She mustered a smile for Thom, and tottered off on killer heels to find Rex, an alternative plan coalescing in the murky depths of her murderous mind.

She knew exactly where to find the old goat: partaking of his evening ritual, sipping cocktails on *Aphrodite's* top deck, watching the spectacular tropical sunset from behind his mirrored sunglasses. Angela shuddered. She was never entirely certain where the ancient letch was looking, but he always made her feel unclean.

Pretending not to see him, Angela sashayed to the gleaming bar and launched into her performance. She poured a line of powder and, leaning from the waist, her pert bottom aimed at Rex, she snorted and swiped her nose back-handed.

She froze when his clammy claws cupped her butt cheeks. He moved shockingly fast and silently for an octogenarian.

"You naughty girl, Angela. Hmm, angel dust? You know I should hand you over to the authorities at the next port?"

Angela slid out of Rex's grasp and pouted. "Why? I'm not hurting anyone."

"Hurting? We could feel good together; share your delectable goodies." Rex leered over the top of his shades.

"I couldn't. If Thom found out, he'd kill me."

"You could do so much better, Angela." Rex ran a gnarled finger under the strap of her bikini top.

Angela pouted. "How much better?"

Rex tapped his flaccid chest. "Infinitely better."

"What's the most dangerous creature you've ever hunted?"

"I've every trophy imaginable. An entire wall filled with glass-eyed heads." Rex sighed. "The novelty wore off decades ago."

"There's one you haven't got. But you wouldn't dare." Angela looked Rex up and down, a brazen challenge to his masculinity. "Marry me, now, and I'll take you manhunting. Here, snort this. Thom's spying on us." She emptied a second baggie on the bar. She leaned and whispered, her moist lips grazed Rex's leathery ear, "It's harmless, I switched it."

Rex hustled Angela to his cabin, where the hastily summoned, blank-faced captain conducted an impromptu marriage ceremony. "I fulfilled my side of the bargain, now it's your turn."

Angela examined the paperwork but discovered no chicanery. "At midnight, we dive. You must pretend to be high. Thom will be waiting, but he won't expect us to attack him. I'll pull off his regulator, you slice his throat. Unfortunately, you can't take his head, it'd be damning evidence. Leave his remains on the seabed."

"You've done this before."

Angela shrugged. "Once or twice."

Rex shivered with anticipation. Angela was far more exciting than expected.

Her plan worked perfectly.

They slid into the bath-warm equatorial waters, and she led Rex to the coral encrusted ravine where her accomplice lurked. Seal sleek in her neon wetsuit, she slid past Thom, whirled around, yanked out his regulator, and wrenched his ponytail. Rex tore open the deckhand's exposed throat and finned backwards as Thom's inky blood stained the water.

Exhilarated, Rex gave a victorious thumbs up as Thom, eyes wide in shock, spasmed and writhed in his death throes. Angela glided to her jubilant new husband and embraced him. Swift and efficient, she gutted Rex with Thom's dropped knife, and tossed his twitching carcass aside for the other ocean predators.

When Angela passed through customs at the next port, she did so as an obscenely wealthy young widow, accompanied by her late husband's loyal captain.

Ransomed

Paper suited strangers wearing goggles and nitrile gloves, crawled over Dr Angela Nightingale's study, collecting hairs and biological matter too small to be noticed without a magnification lens. Dark fingerprint dust marred every flat surface.

The forensics team reminded her of Halloween insect costumes, except this wasn't a party. This was a serious crime scene. The wall safe hung open and her research papers were strewn around the room. The thieves had taken nothing.

But they had left a cheap disposable cell phone in the centre of her desk. Unused, and programmed with one number which the detectives had already established as an unregistered burner.

Detective Inspector Christie cleared his throat. "We're assuming the thieves will make contact using this phone."

Angela tipped her head sideways and waited for pearls of investigative wisdom. None were forthcoming. "I don't think we should use the term thieves, Inspector. They took nothing, except my peace of mind."

Christie shrugged off the comment. "A similar event occurred at your laboratory last week, Doctor. A break-in, but apparently nothing taken? Do you know what they were looking for and who might be responsible?"

A small smile curled Dr Nightingale's lips, and her eyes sparkled. "I'm the keynote speaker at next week's international cancer conference. I will reveal a universal eradication treatment. Whoever is responsible," she waved her hand towards the study, "wants my formula."

"They want to pip you to the post?"

Dr Nightingale frowned. "They want to prevent me from giving the formula to the world. My work will save the lives of millions, but someone wants to block me."

"Who would want to hamper lifesaving medication?" Christie leaned forward.

"Don't they say in the movies, 'follow the money'? Pharmaceutical companies will lose billions when I freely share my methods. No patents, no restrictions."

"Don't you stand to lose money if you give away your work?"

"What's more important, Inspector? Accruing more money than I need, or saving the lives of millions? My legacy will be a cancer free world. I can't put a price on that. Can you?"

Christie nodded towards the study. "How can you tell, from that snowstorm of papers, they didn't get what they came for?"

"Because once I confirmed my findings, I destroyed all written records." Dr Nightingale tapped her temple. "Everything is in here. I don't allow electronic devices in my lab."

"Are your work practises well known?"

"They're not a secret, but I suppose there are those who believe, or hope, I retain a secret hard copy."

"I'll arrange for a team of officers to be with you until the conference. Please don't try to evade them. This is for your protection. They'll be as discrete as possible, but I must assume you are a target."

Tyres slewed to a halt on the gravel driveway, followed by a slammed car door. Running footsteps, then raised voices at the front door.

"My husband, Inspector. I called him immediately after I called you. I'm sure he isn't a risk to my safety and wellbeing."

Christie ambled to the door and Angela listen to muffled voices. Then her husband, Matthew, burst into the room.

"Are you all right? You're not hurt?" Matthew sat beside Angela and draped his arm around her shoulders. He turned to Detective Inspector Christie. "You should be out there, rounding up the local hoodlums."

"We're doing everything we can, sir. Besides, I'm not sure this neighbourhood has any hoodlums. My men will be stationed here until further notice." Detective Inspector Christie nodded and strolled out of the room. He whispered orders to two pairs of constables to remain on the premises and barked commands for the rest to pack up and leave.

Matthew clasped Angela's hands. "We'll pick up Chloe from school and book into a hotel. An impromptu holiday."

"Nonsense. I won't be bullied out of my home. The constables will deter any further incursions. We'll carry on as normal."

Matthew opened his mouth to protest as the burner phone buzzed.

"This must be them." Angela picked up the gadget with the tips of her fingers. "Hello? This is Dr Angela Nightingale. What do you want?"

"You know exactly what I want, Angela." An electronically distorted voice.

"I have nothing to say. I'm hanging up now."

"Wait! Security at your daughter's school is lamentably lax. I'd complain if I was paying those exorbitant fees. Don't worry, Chloe is safe here with me."

Angela blanched, and dropped the phone from nerveless fingers.

Matthew picked it up. "Hello? This is Matthew Nightingale. What do you want?"

"I have Chloe. You are going to exchange your wife for your daughter. I'll be in touch with the details." The phone went dead.

"Phone the school," Angela said, hand over her heart. "They wouldn't hand a child over to just anyone. And Chloe knows better than to go off with a stranger."

Matthew gingerly placed the burner phone on the table and pulled his own phone from his suit pocket. He speed dialled the school.

"Mr Nightingale, I'm so very sorry for your loss," the school receptionist said. Her voice quivered with tears. "Your text came as such a shock. I'm sorry, here I am babbling while you're grieving the loss of your wife. How is Chloe taking the news?"

"I beg your pardon? What text? Angela is here beside me. Where's Chloe?" Matthew's voice rose.

"A policewoman collected her, just as you instructed."

"I didn't send a text."

"I … I have the text right here, Mr Nightingale. I'll put you through to the headmistress."

Matthew hung up. "Someone texted in my name, saying you were dead. The school released Chloe into the care of a policewoman."

"Call the Detective Inspector," Angela said.

The burner phone buzzed with the ferocity of an angry hornet. Matthew glanced at Angela as he reached for the phone. "Hello?"

"You've confirmed we have Chloe? Good. Don't involve the police, not if you want Chloe back alive. Tell Angela what I said."

"They'll kill Chloe if we involve the police," Matthew said.

Angela snatched the phone. "Let me speak to my daughter."

Indistinct shuffles, then ragged breathing. "Mommy? When can I come home?" Chloe whimpered as someone whisked away the phone.

"Chloe's alive. For now. We will ransom your lovely daughter in exchange for you, Dr Nightingale. After you give us the formula, and we've verified your findings, we will release you. A helicopter will arrive in your back garden tonight at eight-thirty. Get rid of the plods." The phone clicked.

Angela frowned and put a finger to her lips. She led Matthew through the French doors into the expansive gardens.

"I think they bugged the house," she said. "Or that blasted phone is also a listening device. They knew we'd spoken to the school. They knew we were about to call the Inspector."

"You can't go," Matthew said. "I won't let you. We'll contact the police and they'll find Chloe. It's what they're paid to do."

"Don't be ridiculous, I'm not risking Chloe's life. We do exactly as they say. First, we have to get rid of the patrolmen."

Matthew scuffed the manicured lawn with his polished toe. "We can't trust these people, Angela."

"We can't afford not to trust them. All I care about is Chloe."

"What about the millions of cancer victims you'll save? Your legacy?"

"Fuck the legacy. Chloe is my only concern." Angela gripped Matthew's wrists. "I'm not responsible for creating cancer. I am responsible for my daughter."

"I'll get rid of the cops. Tell them we're hiring professional bodyguards. No need to waste taxpayer's money."

Angela leaned against the wide trunk of a venerable oak tree. An early scattering of acorns lay between the gnarled roots. "We can't let them win, Matthew. I'm not a fool. I know they have no intention of keeping their word, but I cannot risk Chloe. Regardless of what happens to me, the world deserves the cure."

"That won't happen if you're dead, my love." Matthew knuckled a tear from his eye.

"There's a CD with all the relevant research."

Matthew's eyes grew wide. "Why didn't you tell me?"

"Because knowing puts you in danger. If I don't return, I want you to attend the conference in my stead."

"Where? What …?" Matthew stammered.

"Between the roofing felt and the planks on the rabbit's hutch. I thought nobody would ever think to look there."

Matthew bobbed his head. "I'll … get rid of the uniforms." He jogged back to the house, leaving Angela alone under the oak.

A decade and a half of research, gone. Pouf! As though her career had never been. She trudged back to the house and glared at the burner phone. "If you're listening, you bastard, this isn't over."

She listened as the squad cars crunched down the gravel drive. Unexpectedly, she felt vulnerable. Angela curled up on the deep couch and wept. What if they kill us both? Releasing Chloe would incur unnecessary risks. Whoever they are, they're professionals. Professionals minimise hazards. They'll kill Chloe as soon as they get me. But they might not. Killing a child is a different level of ruthlessness.

A maelstrom of conflicting thoughts swirled in an endless vortex. Angela sat up and took a deep breath. "I will respect the hard-won scientific gains of those physicians in whose steps I walk, and gladly share such knowledge as is mine with those who are to follow." She recited part of the modern Hippocratic oath to an empty room, but the lack of audience did nothing to lessen their meaning. "Louis Lasagna, nothing will prevent me from sharing my findings. And nothing will stop me from rescuing my daughter."

Angela climbed the stairs and drew a bath, vaguely aware Matthew hadn't returned from dismissing the police. She poured in her favourite bubble bath and stirred the foaming water. I might be fucking terrified, but at least I'll smell good. Lavender scents filled the bathroom, but the promised relaxation remained out of reach.

She bathed and redressed in a dark top and trousers with black sneakers, and added an accessory she had never expected to use. Matthew's voice carried from the kitchen, up the stairwell. Angela couldn't discern the words, only the urgency of his tone. "Who were you talking to?" she asked as she entered the kitchen.

Matthew slid his phone into his pocket and gestured to the tray of snacks he had prepared. "No one. You can still change your mind," he said. "We can call the Inspector and set up an ambush."

"An ambush? Wouldn't that guarantee Chloe's death?"

"I feel so bloody helpless. There must be something we can do to ensure you're both safe."

"We must be pragmatic. Make sure my research gets into the right hands. Hope they release Chloe once they have me. That's the best possible outcome. Please don't say anything. I'm clinging to my last scraps of courage because I refuse to give up hope. For Chloe."

The kitchen clock ticked louder than Angela remembered. She pulled it off the wall and yanked out the batteries. The digital clock on the microwave blinked meekly.

"Do you want a drink?"

"Dutch courage? No thanks." Angela folded her arms and leaned on the counter. "As I came down the stairs, I thought I heard you on the phone?"

"Talking to myself." Matthew threw up his hands. "Thinking. Trying to find a solution where I don't lose my wife and daughter."

Angela reached behind her and pulled an old Luger from her pants waistband. She spoke quietly. "My great-grandfather acquired this in the Second World War. If I can't see any other way out, I'll take the bastards with me."

"You're a healer, not a killer." Matthew reached for the pistol.

"I'm a Mother first. I'll destroy anyone who threatens my child." She tucked the gun back under her shirt.

Shadows crept across the garden, and the gloaming assumed an eerie quality.

"Do you think we're under surveillance?" Matthew asked.

"Seems a safe assumption. They'll at least want to know there are no police hiding in the hedges. You sent them all away, didn't you?"

"Of course. We agreed." Matthew stared at the digits flickering on the digital clock. "There's still time to call for help. They could intercept them at the airfield."

"What makes you think they're using an airfield? They're backed by Big Pharma, with limitless budgets. I expect the helicopter will come from a private airfield, and there won't be a flight plan filed anywhere."

"I listened to a debate on the radio recently," Matthew said, his eyes fixed on the kitchen bench.

"Tell me. A distraction would be welcome."

"They were discussing the problems of a growing world population. Someone proposed culling the poorest because they contribute nothing to society." Matthew risked a glance at his wife.

"That's a despicable idea. Anyone who promotes theories like that ought to be locked up."

"Yes, but … he had a point. What I mean is, you still have time to reconsider. To hand over your cure to big pharma. Sure, only the wealthiest will have access, but they're the most worthy of being saved."

"Matthew! Is that what you truly believe?"

He shrugged. "Are your convictions really worth dying for?"

"This breakthrough is bigger than me. Who knows how I or other doctors might expand my work to eradicate other diseases? How could I live with myself if this cure was reserved for the elite, or even worse, completely buried?"

"I'm not like you. I want my wife and daughter to both live, so yes, I'd sacrifice strangers. I'd take the money and live the highlife."

Angela wiped her palms on her thighs. "I'm going to wait in the garden. I need fresh air. Remember, you promised to take the disk to the conference if I don't return." She kissed his cheek and walked out into the cooling evening. The weight of the Luger lent her unmerited confidence. She sat on a stone bench, but couldn't settle and wandered the perimeter of the gardens, her arms goose-pimpling in the cooling air.

Matthew switched off the kitchen lights and pulled the burner phone from his pocket as he watched his wife wandering in the dark. He clicked the pre-programmed number and hesitated. He clenched his jaw and jabbed the send button.

Whoever picked up didn't speak.

"Hello?" Matthew felt his mouth fill with ashes. "Are you there? I have the data. Angela is in the garden. You should have a clear shot." He watched his wife collapse like a marionette with cut stings.

Seconds later, two black-clad balaclava masked figures burst into the kitchen. Matthew's eyes fixed on the silenced gun barrels which filled his entire vision. He didn't feel physical pain, only confusion as he realised he wouldn't be obscenely rich as promised. The double-tap to his forehead was instantaneous. He didn't survive to see the gunmen pick up the disk he'd hidden in the microwave.

Refugees

The toddler pointed excitedly. She'd spied our iridescent wings fluttering feebly against the breeze, too frail to fly any further. The adults shushed her and gave her a rusk to gnaw. They'd stopped believing years ago. Now they were unable to see us. Sadly, their beliefs could soon become our sad reality.

For centuries we retreated from human habitation, seeking sanctuary in the wilderness, but it wasn't enough. Humans ploughed our flowery meadows and razed our sacred woodlands, leaving us homeless and starving. We became refugees.

She tottered in our direction, hands outstretched to grab and squeeze. We cowered, too weak to defend ourselves from this clumsy destroyer. Her mum swooped in and hoisted her onto a maternal hip, chiding her for wandering off, then deposited her within the spurious safety zone of the tartan picnic rug.

The youngling kept her eyes fixed on our fading glamour as she babbled and gurgled to herself. Her chubby fingers dropped the rusk and snatched small handfuls of daisies and buttercups, clovers and dandelions. Our collective anguish knew no bounds as she wantonly harvested our last known food source. Crushing the flowers in her fat fists, she staggered towards our flock and scattered her bounty over us.

Our hopes revived as we sipped the nectar. Energy flooded us, strengthening our rainbow-painted gossamer wings. Grateful for her help, I fluttered closer. Her babbling became more urgent. This green-witchling was speaking the Old Language, guiding us to a place trees and flowers grew year round: what she called a Garden Centre. A magical place to accommodate and feed us until spring.

She advised us to camp over winter and regain our strength. In spring, we can reconnoiter new pastures. She sat hard with a bump, eyes wide with surprise. She giggled, wished us well and manoeuvred onto hands and knees to crawl back to her own kind.

Solstice

Dudda scampered beside his mother as his tribe filed through the forest to the sacred grove, chanting and banging drums to banish evil spirits. Proud in his new winter furs, the suppressed excitement throbbed in his veins.

Adults and children assembled in a ragged circle around the ancient tree, their stamping feet shuddered the earth, their wild music danced along every branch, shimmered on every coppery leaf.

The high priest stood behind the altar, his empty eye sockets searching the crowd. As an acolyte, he'd offered his eyes to the Lord of the Woods, in exchange for the gift of seeing into men's hearts. Dudda dodged behind his mother's wide hips, praying the priest wouldn't point him out as a sinner. Apprehension and a chill wind conspired to make Dudda shiver, despite his layers of fur.

Two priests guided the young girl, a catch from a neighbouring tribe, to the altar. Drugged into compliance, she moved like one already dead. She drank from the offered cup, swallowing mechanically, her face void of all emotion. The brawnier priest held her while the other taped her eyes and mouth with wide strips of leather.

Dudda couldn't decide if making her blind and mute was a mercy to the girl or to the witnesses. He trembled with relief not to be chosen and silently vowed to stay away from their neighbour's borders.

The chanting and stamping grew louder, more rhythmic and insistent, an embodiment of the forest's heartbeat.

The girl collapsed, her red gold hair cascading around her shoulders.

The high priest lifted and carried her to the cleft in the tree. He placed her with all the care of a mother, putting a newborn in her cradle. He muttered unintelligible phrases, deep magic to send this representative of the dying sun to the gods and return reborn at the change of the seasons.

Dudda harboured secret doubts the redhead who would appear at the next solstice would be the same girl, but he didn't care. As long as the sun returned, and as long as he escaped the harvest, then life continued.

The high priest stalked through the swaying crowd and halted next to Dudda. The holy man turned his vacant gaze on the youngster, spearing his soul like a fish in a shallow pond. Dudda clung to his mother's furs, while his heart beat triple time. Cocking his head, as though listening to the forest spirits, the priest slowly smiled and nodded. "I see you," he whispered.

The Christmas Cat

S arah bumped her heels on the chair legs. Poking out her tongue in concentration, she copied out the letter in her best handwriting.

Dear Santa,

Thank you once again for the Giant Book of Fairytales last year. It was smashing. I choose a different bedtime story every night.

We moved house this summer, but Mummy says you'll know where to find us. Our new house doesn't have a chimney. I hope this isn't a problem.

This year I'd like a cat, please, but I don't know how you will deliver one. I am responsible and will feed and brush the cat every day. I promise.

I hope you and the workshop elves are all well.

Please give the reindeer a pat for me. I'll leave out carrots on Christmas Eve.

Love from Sarah.

Sarah and Mummy walked to the Post Office. Sarah posted her letter through the slot, then crossed her fingers all the way home.

On Christmas morning she found an enormous gaily wrapped box, with her name on the label. Santa had found her. She started to tear off the festive paper but remembered she'd told Santa she was responsible, so she gently peeled away the wrapping, careful not to scare the cat inside.

She lifted the flaps and peeped in.

Cat litter and a tray. Boxes of dried cat food and a carton of tiny tins of fish and chicken flavoured cat food. A food bowl and a water dish, decorated with paw patterns. A sparkly cat collar with a dangly jingle bell. A stocking-shaped bag filled with cat toys: things that rolled and clicked, and catnip infused neon coloured feathers on elastic. A kitty grooming kit of brush and claw clippers. Squished at the bottom lay a plush cat bed.

No cat.

Tears trickled down Sarah's cheeks.

"Santa thought I wanted presents for a cat."

"Santa doesn't make mistakes," said Mommy. "Look. What's that envelope?"

The red envelope bearing Sarah's name lay hidden under the wrapping paper.

Dear Sarah,

I couldn't put your cat in my sack. He'd get scared and claw his way out.

He is waiting for you at the shelter.

You will recognise him.

I am glad you are still enjoying your book.

The elves and the reindeers say hello.

Merry Christmas

Santa Claus

Sarah spent the day arranging and rearranging the bed and toys. Mommy helped her clear a shelf in the larder for the food, and to stack the cans.

·•••••••••

Santa must have been very busy, thought Sarah. Lots of other children were collecting their Christmas presents, too.

Sarah gasped. There were kittens galore, but an older striped cat cowered at the back of the enclosure, hissing and sizzling at whoever approached. They blinked slowly at one another. Sarah sat cross-legged and waited patiently. The cat eventually limped forward and clambered onto her lap. He curled up, closed his orange eyes, and rumbled like a train. Sarah caressed his ragged ears and beamed.

"Thank you, Santa. He's absolutely perfect."

Previously published: Chicken Soup For The Soul
October 2020

Liminal Space

Earth.

Here.

Or any other godforsaken backwater colony.

Location makes no difference.

The powerful prey on the weak. An unpleasant human trait.

Rumours circulated for months and still the bodycount rose, authorities reluctant to confront the truth.

The Commander's victims were nobodies. Tiny unclaimed bodies. Nobody's responsibility. Orphans. Runaways. Space trash.

Disposable.

The priest sits in that liminal space, the candle flame flickering. An archaic device on a space station, but the priests love them. Light and dark, life and death. Saints and sinners.

Priest? Are you listening?

Call it serendipity, but before I starved like other underaged undesirables, I discovered my talent. A talent to kill, take a life and slide away unseen. That's why I'm here. After I made a fortune selling my skills to the highest bidder, I heard the rumours.

Why? Why did I care?

I could have been one of those victims, way back when I was young and vulnerable.

Guilt? Why should I feel guilt?

If I didn't do it, someone else would. Someone less skilled. Do you know what that means, Priest? It means a messier, more painful death. I was quick, clean, merciful. I took no satisfaction or pleasure from inflicting pain. My fees didn't include torture or rape. I didn't provide those services.

I shuffle my feet, rattling my irons, my ankles chafed and bleeding.

Shall I tell you a secret, Priest? Will it satisfy your vicarious lust?

The cleric rearranges his robes, nodding as the flame dances in his hungry eyes.

Very well. Closer, lean closer.

I took my time with The Commander, ignored my own rules. I enjoyed every second of his agony. Each incision was exquisite, each break a work of art. I made him pay for every bairn he abused. He experienced the pain and terror he'd inflicted on each defenceless runaway. His screams were payment. The blood, snot, piss, and shit were welcome bonuses.

Why didn't I escape? Why surrender to the Authorities?

Because this is the first time I've felt pride.

The candle gutters. When it dies, I will be executed. No matter. I've lived far longer than I could reasonably have expected and enjoyed wealth beyond my wildest dreams. I have no regrets.

I stare, mesmerised by the flame. My life is burning away, steadily, inexorably. The ghosts of the orphans call to me, thanking me for avenging them, promising to keep me company in the cold empty void of space.

The wax spreads, a hot greasy puddle. The priest stands, offering to bless me. I wave him away. A hypocrite who thrilled at my description of mutilation, rigid with desire at the mention of abuse. He slaps the button, opens the airlock door and passes to safety. He has done his job. Unrepentant, I am assigned to oblivion. I shuffle to the outer door, waiting to join my beloved unloved.

The candle snuffs. Darkness envelopes me. A silent scream is torn from my lungs as the void welcomes me.

I am space trash.

Previously published: Galaxy 2

May 21

The Memorial Ring

Crashing thunder accompanies the deluge of rain, which splatters high off the pavement, forcing me to shelter in the dingy antique shop. I hesitate on the threshold, allowing my eyes to adjust to the dim light. A set of chimes announces my entrance and a wind gust slams the door behind me. I glance through the unwashed windows, the pyrotechnics of the storm are in full force.

I hang my sunglasses from the neck of my shirt and look around. Heavy furniture laden with object d'art whose value I cannot guess cluster around me. I drift aimlessly to the rear of the shop and spy the jewellery counter. The glass sparkles from a recent polish, contrasting with the rest of the shop, which looks like it hasn't been so much as dusted in decades. The modern LED lighting is out of place but draws me in.

Each meticulously displayed piece is accompanied by a small handwritten label. Not the jumbled heap I was expecting. A large ring sits pride of place and I bend for a closer look, squinting to read the description. My involuntary gasp is shockingly loud and I glance around, hoping I haven't disturbed anybody. The establishment is empty of both customers and staff. I hunch over again to read the spidery writing.

The Georgian era ring honours a man's wife and two children. A centre plait of silver-blond hair belonged to the wife, the ebony-dark thinner plaits on either side are from their children. Outer rows of alternating seed pearls and tiny rubies symbolise tears and a broken heart. Black enamel represents death. I can see no price on the ring, but every other item has a prominent price tag.

Wearing the hair of dead people as jewellery strikes me as creepy, but I am enchanted by this ring. I place my hand on the counter, assessing whether it is small enough to fit my middle finger.

"It's not for you, you don't want that, you don't. How about one of these pretty carved coral rings?"

"Fuck! You scared the bejeezus out of me. I didn't see you. Umm, sorry. You … you scared me."

"Not me you need to fear. Now, how about one of these pretty little pieces, eh? Much more suitable …"

"Is this ring for sale? I've read the description but I can't see a price tag. What can you tell me?"

Clearly reluctant, the wizened man opens the glass counter, his gnome-like hand hovering uncertainly over the memorial ring.

"Are you sure you wouldn't like … ?"

"No. I'd like to see this one, please. It's very unusual. Dramatic. May I try it on? I think it'll be too big, though." As I reach out to take the ring, I notice the little man trembling. *Parkinson's? That would explain why the place looks neglected.* He drops the ring onto my upturned palm. The weight surprises me.

I inspect the ring. There are no signs of wear. *Maybe wearing it was too upsetting.* The tightly plaited hair looks metallic. I would have guessed silver and black rhodium. The seed pearls and rubies are exquisite. Sliding the ring onto my middle finger, I feel a grin split my face. A perfect fit. I hold up my hand to the overhead lights, twisting it this way and that, watching the light play over the varied surfaces.

"I love it!"

The man looks displeased, not at all what I expect.

"There's a story here, do you know any more about this piece? Anything?"

I can't help but hold up my hand to admire the ring and marvel. The ring could have been tailor made for me. Who'd have thought a specially commissioned ring over two hundred years old would be a perfect fit?

"I know it's bad luck, that ring. Every owners been driven mad, no one keeps it for long … it always returns. I'm sorry, I shouldn't have let you try it on. It's not suitable, not for you. Too much tragedy attached to that ring."

I laugh. "Really? You're saying this ring is … what? Cursed? C'mon, you don't believe that. I don't. You don't need to spin me a spooky sales pitch, I've already said I love it. What's the asking price?"

"There is no 'asking price', it's priceless." Cocking his head, he smiles sadly. "Can you take it off, or is it stuck?"

"If you don't want to sell it, you shouldn't have it on display." I tug angrily at the ring. "Sod it! I didn't realise it was this tight. D'you have soap? Something to lubricate it?" I continue twisting and tugging the ring.

"Stop! You'll hurt yourself. Stop. The ring has chosen you, my dear."

"Soap, a bit of soap or hand cream will get it off." Tears rise unbidden, blurring my vision. I swipe at my eyes. "Priceless, you said. I can't afford an expensive ring. Help me get it off."

"You misunderstood, Miss." He reaches over, cradling my bejewelled hand between his gnarled fingers. "Priceless means without a price, the ring has chosen you, don't you see? You slipped it on easily enough; the size isn't the issue. The ring is yours now." Clutching my hand, he circles the counter and leads me through the shop. "Be on your way. The ring will make it back here when it's ready." Opening the door with his free hand, he propels me out and shuts the door behind me. The chimes celebrate my exit.

I rattle the now locked door. He smiles and turns his back.

· · • · • · • · · ·

The storm has passed, and the pavement is steaming, wisps of vapour dancing and evaporating. I reach my car without anyone chasing after me, denouncing me as a thief. The huge ring now spins freely around my finger. I slip it off and back on, unable to figure out the jest.

I slow down as I approach the shop. I'll hop out and return the ring. A clever hoax, most entertaining. The shop is in darkness; the door locked. I cup my hands to peer through the grimy windows, then step backwards to look up and down the street. I must have the wrong shop. This one is empty.

· · • · • · • · · ·

I keep the ring on when I climb into bed, weirdly satisfied by its weight. *Of course, the ring is a modern fake. That explains why there are no signs of wear. He probably buys them by the carton from China and amuses himself performing silly parlour tricks on unsuspecting customers. Sneaky old bugger!*

··•·•·•••·

Gasping for breath, I struggle awake and push the pillow from my face. I take huge gulps of air as I stare wild-eyed around my room. I flick on the bedside lamp, nothing lurks in the corners. The bathroom is equally devoid of intruders. Tepid water straight from the tap soothes my throat. Nothing under the bed. Muttering imprecations at my foolishness, I climb in and pull the covers to my chin. My thumb rotates the ring around my middle finger. *Bloody charlatan!*

··•·•·•••·

I awake exhausted, having lost track of how many times I woke, panicked and gasping for breath. Being spooked by a silly trick is beneath me. I place the antique style ring on my bedside table.

While brushing my teeth after a rushed breakfast, I select my clothes. My charcoal pantsuit and cream silk tee shirt worn with the ruby red and black scarf will be perfect with my new ring. There's no rational reason to resist. I accessorise with silvery flats and bag.

··•·•·•••·

My friends laugh at my story, agreeing the shop owner tricked me. They examine the ring and pronounce it a very attractive fake.

··•·•·•••·

Refusing to be intimidated, I wear the ring to bed. I have already formed an unconscious habit of twisting it around with my thumb. I fall asleep quickly, last night's lack of sleep catching up with me.

The snick of the lock jolts me awake. I hear the familiar creak of hinges and the careful pad of bare feet. The tall figure lunges at me, his superior weight bearing me down. My screams wake me. Sobbing and shaking, I tear the ring from my finger and fling it across the room. I curl into a foetal position and drag the covers over my head. Claustrophobia drives me back out to breathe. I flick on the bedside lamp, childishly feeling safer.

I succumb to fitful sleep, disturbed countless times by dreams of someone hissing "Sara". *Who the hell is Sara?*

Sara McGowen. The name has been finger painted with toothpaste on my bathroom mirror. A quick check of the house reveals nothing: no sign of forced entry, doors and windows locked. The police respond quickly to my frantic call; they take photographs and dust for fingerprints, including mine for elimination. An officer conducts a security check but finds nothing. They leave, reminding me to keep my doors and windows locked. *Locks didn't stop someone last night!*

I remember flinging the ring across the bedroom, but there it sits on my bedside table, no doubt placed there by one of the police officers. Picking up the ring, I am once again awed by the exquisite workmanship. Not what I'd expect from a cheap Chinese knockoff. Before I realise what I'm doing, the ring is snug on my finger and I'm staring at the name on the mirror.

An internet search of Sara McGowen reveals nothing useful, but the town library archives may be more fruitful. The formidable elderly librarian who appears to have sole charge directs me to the bowels of the building. She explains they are working backwards, digitising their records, but documents from the early 1800s remain boxed up, more or less in date order. She gives me a piercing look and strict instructions about the rules.

I wander aimlessly, picking and exploring boxes at random, with no idea where to start, nor what to look for. I am wasting my time. *I've had enough, I'm going!* Without warning, the ring slips from my finger and rolls purposefully down the corridor of stacked boxes, abruptly stopping next to an unlabelled box. Stooping warily, I collect the ring, slipping it back where it is once again a snug fit.

The box is large but surprisingly light. I carry it to the table. Inside is a jumble of personal items: a handwritten book, a bundle of letters tied with faded pink ribbon, and a sketchbook are the most interesting. I start with the handwritten book, thinking it is a diary. It's a collection of herbal remedies recorded in different handwriting, all of which are hard to decipher. Someone has pressed flowers and leaves between the pages. The letters addressed to Sara are filled with protestations of undying love from Edward. He includes vividly erotic poetry. I blush and refasten the pink ribbon. The fragile pages of the sketchbook are a revelation. The first pages are pencil studies of a swarthily handsome unsmiling man. Sara had a gift for portraiture. Her self portrait looks alive, the lips about to laugh. Lively sketches of babies and toddlers crowd the following pages. The sorrow in her next self portrait is devastating. *What has wiped away all her joy, and made her fearful?* The handsome man features again, looking cruel and frustrated. There are no more pictures of children. Sara obsessively drew a dark-haired, full-figured woman with a haughty expression. The latter half of the sketchbook is filled with sketches of her. The passion with which they were destroyed is evident by the holes gouged through the paper.

·········

Wretched and grief stricken, I awake sobbing for my drowned babies sleeping in the family vault in tiny twin coffins. Despite what Edward told me, I know it was no accident. I will be next. When he loved me, he declared I had enchanted him, but none of my spells or potions will save me now. Death will bring reunion with my darlings and I will be rid of that hateful woman with whom Edward plans to replace me.

·········

My dream filled night has left me debilitated. Edward soured after the birth of their children, turning his attention to a mistress. He returned from the lake bearing the drowned bodies of both children, claiming an accident. No one questioned his story or his stoic grief. When Sara voiced her disbelief, Edward declared her hysterical and locked her in her room, only allowing her out to visit the vault where her sleeping angels rested. He kept her sedated by spiking her food and drink. He encouraged her to take her own life, only her fear of never being reunited with her babies in Heaven prevented her committing a mortal sin. She comforted herself by plaiting the fine dark hair of her babies along with her own. She sent the plaits with a sketch of her design to Edward's jeweller. Every piece of jewellery with which Edward had plied her had come from this master craftsman.

By the time the commission was complete, Sara was dead.

Impatient to remarry, Edward suffocated her with a pillow. Friends and neighbours were unsurprised to learn Edward's delicate wife had succumbed to grief. The ring and accompanying bill arrived the morning of her funeral. The appeal to Edward's twisted humour was too great to resist. He wore the ring at the funeral, ostentatiously twisting it around his pinkie finger while receiving condolences with the haughty woman possessively by his side. Edward laid Sara to rest next to her babies. He laid the ring to rest in the jeweller's box.

· · · • · • • • · · ·

I find the shop easily enough, although it looks smarter than I remember, with gleaming windows and shiny brass door furniture.

"I didn't expect you back so soon." The old man looks bashful.

"You knew Sara's story, didn't you? That's why you didn't want me to have the ring."

"I knew Sara, I loved her. I made the ring …"

"Hold on, please, I'm coming." The vibrant voice distracts me, and I look towards the back of the store. A stylish middle-aged woman bustles towards me. "So sorry to keep you waiting, how can I help?"

"No, that's fine. This gentleman …" I gesture to empty space. "I was talking to an older gentleman, he helped me a few days ago with this ring." I frown, confused by his disappearance. I didn't think he could move that fast. "He was just here …"

"I'm the only one working here, lovey. Never had an assistant. You must be mistaken. May I see the ring?"

I extend my hand, expecting her to accuse me of theft.

"Georgian, I think. Unusual … beautiful workmanship. Are you looking to sell it? I can always buy quality items." She smiles hopefully at me.

The ring tightens imperceptibly on my finger.

· · · • · • • • · ·

Last night I slept peacefully. My thumb automatically spins the ring, which moves freely. The finger painted toothpaste message this morning reads: Thank you & Blessed be.

The Organ Donor

Liza lost track of time much faster than she'd expected, but she blamed the cocktail of hallucinogenics they'd stabbed into her leg after bundling her into the back of an unmarked black van, wrapped in the electrified catch-net. Her thigh still throbbed.

Dry mouthed and disoriented, she listened as a phalanx of booted personnel tramped down the narrow concrete corridor, but reasoned they could only be a small group. The footsteps faded as they passed her locked cell door.

Eventually they'd stop.

Liza had witnessed the mutilated women unceremoniously dumped back in the wild. Physically wrecked, emotionally traumatised, and incapable of independence, they begged for merciful deaths. She silently cursed her arrogance. The squirrels she'd been hunting were not worth the inevitable cost.

The Stygian darkness was punctuated by eyeball searing brightness at random times for unguessable periods. Liza assumed they had her under biometric surveillance. She counted her breaths in and out, deliberately calm, determined to offer no exploitable weakness. Except for the obvious. The reason she'd been captured. She failed to suppress a shudder.

Blood seeped from wrists and ankles rubbed raw by the heavy shackles securing her to the cruelly cold metal chair. She unclenched her fists and wiggled her fingers and naked toes.

Careful footsteps, freighted with purpose, slowed as they approached her cell. Overhead lights gently hummed to life, far removed from the earlier savage blazes. The locking mechanism clicked like a disapproving elder, and an elegantly suited woman strode through the door, her glossy smile as fake as her nail extensions.

The woman tutted and snapped her fingers for a hovering attendant to dress the oozing wounds. "We must take care of you, Liza. You're far too valuable to mistreat." She purred with the sincerity of a well-fed cat. "You don't mind if I use your first name? We'll be together for a long time and we ought to be on friendly terms. I'm Olivia."

Liza glared.

Olivia sucked her lip and nodded. "No doubt you've heard fanciful stories, but a healthy woman like you should be pleased to perform her civic duty. And it's better than being worked to death in a factory, or dying in the fields. You'll be well treated."

"Fuck you!"

"You'll have to join the back of a long queue for that particular pleasure." Olivia raised a perfect eyebrow. "But it's not entirely out of the question."

An assistant projected a digital album onto the wall. Men, middle-aged to elderly, plump with prosperity and sleekly self-important.

"This is a great opportunity for someone like you," Olivia said. "Choose one with whom to mate and, if you find favour, you'll be allowed access to the child you bear, and will receive a monthly stipend as an honoured mother of an elite child. Or refuse and we will harvest your ovaries and whatever other organs are currently in demand. You'll be returned to the wilderness to survive as best you can. Your choice."

The Orphaned Ring

I fly out of the store and slow to a regular shopper shuffle, small steps, blank face, no rush, no urgency, nothing to call attention to myself. The Saturday shopping crowd engulfs me.

A stupid spontaneous theft. Sloppy. Idiotic. Unprofessional.

What possessed me? I have no buyer lined up and I wouldn't be caught dead wearing it. A teardrop shaped blue sapphire surrounded by diamonds? Too Princess Di. Exquisite craftsmanship, quality gems, but not my style. A ring I don't like and can't fence, at least not until the hullabaloo dies.

I dodge down a laneway, turn my jacket inside out, and shake loose my hair. It's a start. If I'm caught for something so bloody stupid, I'll never live it down.

After zigging and zagging, I emerge in the restaurant district, where tables spill with artful abandon across sun-warmed pavements. Succulent cooking odours and live music compete for attention. Bags hooked over chair backs gape open, a treasure trove of contents for all to see. I swipe a pair of heavy-rimmed glasses and push out the lenses. Super man in reverse. I slide into a chair at a recently vacated table, pick up the abandoned latte, and feign fascination with my phone.

The store detectives are rank amateurs. Red faced, thick legged, and flabby bellied, they crash through thickets of seating.

Security never looks for someone relaxing after a meal; they look for a panicked runner. They pass me in a self-important cloud of radio chatter.

I surreptitiously abandon the orphaned ring in the coffee dregs, hoist my zipped shoulder bag and melt away.

Moving On

Annie hunched her shoulders against the chill wind slicing between the headstones and trudged on, as she had every Wednesday afternoon for the last forty weeks. Gravel crunched underfoot, the sound muffled by the swirling fog which clung damply to her winter coat in a fine glaze that glistered under the randomly placed lampposts.

What if he isn't here? Only an idiot would traipse about in this blasted weather. Annie shoved her gloved hands deep into her coat pockets, chrysanthemums crushed unceremoniously under her arm. *At least if he's not here, he'll not see my embarrassment. He won't know meeting him every week is the highlight of my miserable life.*

Her father's grave was the most well-tended in the cemetery. Every week she brought fresh flowers, trimmed the grass with scissors she kept in her 'grave bag', and raked the blue-grey gravel free of weeds. She kept a selection of rags for polishing the headstone.

Annie dumped her 'grave bag' and the bunch of 'mums at the foot of the plot and removed her gloves with her teeth. Trying not to be obvious, she scanned the area for her friend as she emptied and refilled the vase. *Don't be so bloody gormless, woman. He won't be here in this filthy weather.*

Annie arranged the creamy blooms to her satisfaction, hiding the crushed ones at the back, and gave the marble headstone a cursory wipe. She stepped back to admire the floral display glowing against the black stonework.

"You do him proud, Annie."

You came. "Thank you, Ben. I didn't expect to see you today, what with it being so miserable."

Ben shrugged his wide shoulders. "I wanted to see you."

"Coffee? I brought a flask and sandwiches, on the off chance you'd be here." Annie smiled shyly. A picnic under the pagoda had become their weekly ritual.

Ben offered his arm, an old world courtesy which charmed Annie. She wasn't a woman to whom tall, handsome men offered their arm. He steered her through the roiling banks of fog as though crossing a Spring meadow. he laid his muffler on the bench with a gallant flourish.

Annie noticed the droplets of moisture clinging to his eyelashes. *Why is it always men blessed with the longest, thickest lashes?* She felt the heat rise in her when she realised he was watching her.

"I'm sorry, I didn't mean to stare," Annie said. "I was admiring your eyelashes. Most women would die for such long, thick lashes." *Shut up, shut up, shut up. He'll think you're simple minded, prattling on about bloody eyelashes.*

"Aye," Ben said, as he poured coffee from the flask. "They are womanish."

"No, I didn't mean it like that. They're beautiful. I'm jealous." Annie turned away, certain the heat she felt in her cheeks flamed brightly for all the world to see. She gulped the scalding coffee to stop her mouth from running away with her.

Ben hummed quietly as he cradled his coffee. He paused every few bars to inhale the rich aroma. Annie noticed he didn't eat much for such a big man. Her father would have chided him for playing with his food. Each week, at least half his sandwich fed the sparrows and pigeons whose favourite haunt was the memorial gardens.

Annie gulped her coffee and gobbled her food when she was nervous. Sitting with Ben, she felt like a gauche schoolgirl. She gulped and gobbled like a starving gannet, becoming more hideously self-conscious with each convulsive swallow. She brushed the crumbs off her lap to a flurry of excited sparrows.

Ben smiled his wide, slow smile. "Does a man good to see a woman with a healthy appetite."

Is he laughing at me? Is that a polite way of saying I'm fat? Annie sucked in her belly, knowing full well it'd collapse back when she spoke. *I'm joining the gym. Not for Ben; for me. I should look after my health.*

"You don't each much. I suppose grief does that to a body. No accounting for how folk respond to the death of a loved one." *Did I really say that? Ooh, that was trite. Keep your mouth shut, Annie. You sound more intelligent that way.*

Fitful gusts of wind shredded the fog and cut through Annie's coat, chilling her to the bone. She clamped her jaw closed to stop her teeth from chattering.

"Are you cold, Annie?"

She shivered and nodded, not trusting herself to speak.

"Come on, let's walk. Warm up your blood." Ben gathered the picnic remains into the bag and offered his arm to Annie.

"Y'know, in all these months you've never shown me which grave," Annie said.

Ben faltered. Annie wouldn't have noticed if she hadn't been holding his arm. *There you go, putting your foot in it again. Why did I automatically assume a parent's grave? I bet it's his wife's, the love of his life, and he's still consumed with grief. He's only being nice to me because he's naturally polite.* Annie slipped her arm free from Ben and instantly felt bereft.

Ben glanced sideways at her, but stayed silent.

Should I make the first move? How long does grief last before it becomes an unhealthy obsession? "Much as I enjoy our chats under the pagoda each week, it's getting a bit chilly, don't you think?"

"I understand. You've done more than most, but now's the time to move on. I'll miss you, Annie, more than you'll ever know."

"I thought next week, if you like, you could come to my place. For lasagne, nothing fancy - maybe a bottle of wine?"

"I don't know if I can do that, Annie. I'm not sure I can get away."

"Not sure you can get away? You're married, aren't you? Here I was, thinking you're grieving for the love of your life, but you're still married. How could you?"

"No, no, you've got it wrong. You don't understand."

"I understand all too well. Your wife doesn't understand you? You live separate lives? Don't bother; I've heard it all before. I thought you were different."

Annie snatched back her bag and set off for the cemetery gates. Half blind with tears of shame and self pity, she hurtled onto the road.

She sat up, dazed. Ben raced towards her, a crowd of strangers behind him.

"Annie, Annie. I didn't want it to be like this. I didn't know how to tell you without scaring you." Ben helped her to her feet and brushed her down, the growing crowd murmuring around them.

Who are these people? Where did they come from? "I'm fine, really. Please don't fuss." Annie glanced around for her bag. Her hands flew to her mouth, stifling a rising wail of fear when she saw her corpse lying broken at her feet.

Ben wrapped his arms around her, offering what comfort he could.

Annie recoiled. *I'm dreaming, I've been knocked unconscious and I'm having one of those out-of-body experiences. This isn't real.*

A commotion at the back of the crowd distracted her.

"Let me through, outta my way. That's my daughter. Let me through."

"Dad?"

Annie's dad placed his hands on her shoulders. "Annie, my love, I see Ben beat me to it. Good man you've got there. He's pestered me nonstop about you since the day of my funeral. Persistent bugger. Love at first sight, he said."

"Walk with me, Annie?" Ben offer his arm, "I've something to show you."

Annie's dad gave her a gentle push, and she slipped her arm through Ben's and walked back through the gates. The sirens and flashing lights from the emergency vehicles converging on her body faded. The dank fog melted as sunlight flooded the cemetery and a carpet of flowers blossomed underfoot. A warm breeze carried birdsong across the memorial gardens.

"Here." Ben pointed to a modest headstone carved with his name and dates. No family members. "This is my grave. You startled me earlier, I thought you'd guessed. I couldn't accept your invitation because I'm not sure how far I can travel and maintain a corporeal presence. And I don't know what 'lasagne' means." Ben raised an inquiring eyebrow.

Annie ran her fingers over the dates, doing the maths in her head. "You're a fair bit older than me, aren't you?"

"Does it matter?"

"No. Not one iota."

Annie stepped into his embrace amidst cheers from the other residents who drifted after them.

"Can we find somewhere more private?" Annie whispered in Ben's ear, eager to skip the frozen dinner and cheap plonk stage of their romance.

Digging Up The Past

Tourists spill from the chartered bus, and are swallowed by the gaping mouth of the fossil and crystal shop. Barrels and bins overflow like pirate's booty. Displays of loose tumble stones and jagged crystals of unimaginable variety are artfully lit, each promising improbable physical and mental health benefits. Bracelets and necklaces cover the walls, and fragile shell mobiles tinkle in the air-conditioned breeze.

Silver set rings and brooches, under gleaming glass counters, lure the group down the preordained path of retail therapy. Clusters of dragon eggs perch on wooden plinths. I hesitate by the amber, enthralled by the lumps of fossilised tree sap. From milky white to golden honey; from mossy green to glossy black; the polished chunks beg sweaty holidaymakers to trail sticky fingers over their smooth coolness.

Against my will, I am drawn into a faux cavern encrusted with sparkling gems, where a spotty youth offers geodes for us to split with miniature hammers. He demonstrates the technique, revealing miraculous interiors glittering with guaranteed treasure. My travel companions hand over cash in exchange for the opportunity to smash rocks. Their squeals of delight bounce off the walls like red cordial infused children at a birthday party.

I escape the group and steal into a dimly lit grotto. An entire wall is devoted to ammonites. Their Cretaceous spirals curl defensively. Tiny delicate shells smaller than my fingernail, to massive armoured tank specimens; sand pale to coal black, matt to iridescent. I wince at the mirror image of the sliced fossil, buffed and mounted to display where once tender innards resided. Mesmerised, my fingers trace the intricate spiral, inner to outer, juvenile to maturity. As the prehistoric creatures grew, they extended their shells and moved into the new section, their past sealed behind them.

An entire life mapped in stone. Private made public; development as entertainment.

A physical representation of my life: spiralling from child prodigy to raddled addict. Each episode of my life carefully outgrown and sealed, then exposed by the media in centrefolds and full-colour specials. Every failed relationship, each drug fuelled embarrassment, sliced open and laid out in lurid detail for public analysis, while I groped to make sense of my fantasy existence.

I nod at the eager assistant and gesture with my credit card. She reverently folds tissue over the exposed sections, wrapping and bagging my spontaneous purchase in protective layers. I cradle the package with quasi-religious care.

How can I safeguard my privacy as effectively as the layers of tissue and bubble wrap protect the fossil?

Last Wishes

The end of the tape flutters: a fragile flag of victory, describing endless flickering circuits. I press the stop button and stare at the smug bastard sitting opposite. Cockatoos squabble in the nearby palms and a skink watches us with basilisk curiosity.

"Who else knows?"

He tips back his straw trilby with one finger. "Only you and me, babe."

Babe? Goosebumps shiver over my skin. I detest smarmy terms of endearment and I really fucking hate this asshole who thinks he can manipulate me.

"Who else has a copy?"

"Nobody, babe. This is between us. Once we recover the diamonds, we can buy a tropical island, a condo in New York, do anything we please."

"You don't need me. You can hire a boat and divers for a pittance. Keep the billions all to yourself."

He nods at the tape deck. "You heard your old man. He said you should take care of me. Surely you wouldn't deny your father's last wishes?"

No, I won't deny Dad's dying request. I'll do exactly as he suggested. I sniff and reach inside my cavernous handbag. "Hay fever," I say. My fingers close around the tiny Beretta Pico. "Did Dad show you a map?"

He pulls a much folded piece of paper from his shirt pocket and waves it in the air. "We're going to the Maldives, babe."

I cringe at the endearment, but my aim is true. A tiny hole blossoms between his eyes. Blood seeps onto the useless map. He was right about the Maldives, but not the sunken treasure crap. Dad fucking hated the water. The ice is in a numbered account. The number my old man clicked out in Morse Code while this asshole interrogated him.

"Thanks, Dad." I don my outsize sunnies and stroll away, leaving the putz baking in the sun. "I took care of him, just as you suggested."

So Help Me, God

The village of Little Badger Dropping possessed few tourist attractions. The crumbling Norman church of Blessed Ethelred with its squat square tower and overgrown weed ridden cemetery drew a few tweedy history buffs, who dutifully completed the wax rubbings and gleefully escaped next door to the black and white timbered pub for a traditional cottage pie or a ploughman's with homemade pickles.

Misshapen cottages, bulging beneath thatched roofs, huddled around the village green. Four-wheel drives and luxury sedans signalled the invasion of well-heeled outsiders. They wore new waxed jackets and unscuffed green wellies on their weekend-in-the-country jaunts. A mariachi band and neon lights couldn't have more clearly marked them as townies.

Reverend "call me Pete" wept. No amount of creative accounting could disguise the horror. The village was dying.

He sank to his knees and prayed for guidance. For a wealthy benefactor to fund the church roof replacement. Unimpressed by Reverend Pete's plight, his God remained stubbornly silent. Which doesn't mean Reverend Pete didn't hear a sympathetic voice whispering an ungodly solution.

He held mass in an empty church. Townies preferred to worship at The Cat and Fiddle, with unconsecrated sparkling wine and artisanal sourdough bread.

Reverend "call me Pete" lurked in the shadows of the millennium old yew trees at the church gate. He shivered as their black leaves rustled forbidden stories of pagan sacrifices, of ancient practices, and exacting long forgotten gods.

The sozzled townie staggered out of the pub and puked over Pete's brogues. That disrespectful act sealed his fate. Sacrificial knives belonged to long gone eras, so Pete plunged a cheese knife into his victim's neck. With more luck than judgement, he nicked the carotid artery.

As Pete expected, a local dog walker found the exsanguinated remains.

The media descended on the village like hounds on an injured fox. They interviewed everyone, as each reporter sought an angle, a personal story.

Reverend "Call me Pete" invited television crews into his dilapidated church. Without blaming the newbies, he described the slow, painful death of the village, and the necessity of an infusion of fresh blood to ensure the community's survival.

The pews overflowed, leaving standing room only at the next mass. Tourists gathered near the yew-shaded gate and snapped selfies.

Reverend Pete's prayers were answered. The old gods appreciated their new convert.

Donations flooded in from across the country. Enough to fund a new church roof.

Snapper King

The cosmic orange kombi-van, spattered with midnight blue and sun yellow cartoon daisies, jounced down the rutted trail. Hans squinted through the dusty windscreen as he wrestled the steering wheel.

"Why did we come this way?" Chloe asked. "I'm sure this is a dead end."

A frill-necked lizard darted out of the brush and raced ahead of them before cutting back into the tinder-dry undergrowth.

Hans pointed to a rusted roof sheltering under straggly eucalyptus trees. "All tracks lead somewhere." An ominous bang preceded the spout of steam which escaped from the overworked rear engine. The van lurched and limped to the front porch of The Snapper King Hotel, and settled with a sigh into the dirt like a roosting bush turkey.

Nature was hard at work reclaiming the split logs and corrugated iron, an effort seemingly unrivalled by the property owners. Long and low, the aged building squatted like a crocodile on a mudbank.

Cicadas, invisible and impossibly loud, welcomed the backpackers. Humidity wrapped them in an uncomfortably damp and intimate embrace. The hand-painted banner above the pub door, welcoming competitors both local and international, sagged under the joint weight of tropical heat and heavy responsibility. "Welcome to the Snapper King International Quarter Century Snap Competition."

Chloe looked for evidence of other tourists. "Snap? The kid's card game? I don't see any other cars or vans."

Hans cranked the motor. Not a rumble. Not even an asthmatic cough. "I guess we're gonna be here for a few days. This old girl isn't moving." He tapped the console. "Shall we splurge on a room rather than a campsite?"

Chloe leaned across and pecked his cheek. "In this instance, I thoroughly approve of your middle-class conservative sensibilities."

They peeled themselves from the sweaty vinyl seats and trudged up the rickety steps of the pub. A blast of air-conditioned decadence raised goosebumps on their skin. They tugged their meagre clothing from their sticky torsos and headed for the unattended but surprisingly well-stocked bar.

The rear wall mirror sparkled, glasses gleamed, and framed photographs shone under the dim lights. Every picture, sepia, black and white, and colour, showed people clutching playing cards. Their expressions ranged from gleeful to terrified.

"That your van out front?" The raspy voice startled the backpackers. A man in a faded checkered shirt and frayed stubbies appeared in the mirror's reflection. He rounded the bar and polished with a spotless tea-towel the smudged patch where they'd both leaned. "You can't park there."

Hans stuck out his hand. "Hi, I'm Hans and this is my girlfriend, Chloe. Klara the Kombi seems to have carked it. I'm hoping you can recommend a mechanic."

"Louie." He ignored the proffered hand. "Back in my day, you could fix those things with a rubber band or a wad of chewing gum. No mechanics or repair shops hereabouts."

"Can we use your telephone?" Chloe waggled her mobile. "No service out here."

The cicada orchestra stopped without warning. Louie growled into the depths of the ensuing silence. "Who're you gonna call?"

"The nearest tow truck operator," Chloe said. She kicked Hans in the ankle, below Louie's range of sight.

Louie frowned. "You'll not get a towie out here for love nor money. You're better off waiting until after the game and cadging a lift. Assuming you still plan to leave."

Chloe laughed. "We can't stay here forever."

"We'll see," Louie said. "A double room, I presume?"

Hans drew his credit card. "Do you need any other ID? Driver's licence?"

"Why? You planning on hoofing it through the bush?" Louie reached for a key with a Joker playing card plastic fob. "I'll show you to your room. You can settle in before dinner. The restaurant opens at six."

Hans and Chloe followed Louie to a ramshackle bungalow which hadn't enjoyed the attention of a maintenance worker for many seasons. Louie snicked the key into the lock and revealed a clean but spartan room.

Chloe waited until Louie was out of earshot before turning to Hans. "Did you clock his expression when I asked to use the phone? Must have been a trick of the light, but I could swear his eyes glowed red."

"You've watched too many tacky B movies. Louie's probably not used to customers. He's a bit of a weirdo. Lacks social skills."

"He runs a pub. Social skills are the primary prerequisite. And you can't say weirdo. Eccentric individual is acceptable."

Hans shrugged. "Let's hope our eccentric host's restaurant is as good as his bar. You want to jump in the shower while I fetch our bags?"

Chloe shook her head. "I'll come with you. We can shower together." She winked to cover her feeling of dread.

Together, they collected their bundles of clothing and toiletries, and scampered back to their room, giggling like children.

"Did you notice the sign was down?" Chloe asked. "Maybe Louie's cancelled because nobody turned up. Looks like we're the only guests."

"Not much point having a sign, if you think about it," Hans said. "Apart from a passing goanna or a curious kangaroo, who's gonna see?"

By the time they had freshened up and returned to the pub, Louie had set a table with blinding white linen and glittering glasses. A white native orchid stood in a crystal bud-vase.

Louie pulled out their seats. "Lasagna's in the oven. Be about another ten minutes. What can I get you folks to drink?"

"I'm not sure I fancy lasagna," Chloe said. "May I see the menu?"

"Menu? Ain't got a menu. I've defrosted the lasagna specially for you. I can bring you a drinks menu, though."

"Two sparkling waters, please." Hans glanced at Chloe, who shrugged.

"Ice?"

"Yes, please," Chloe said.

Louie strode away, tea-towel over his arm. He returned with two frosty glasses of fizzy water and a saucer of sliced lemons. "No wine?"

Chloe shook her head, and Louie gathered the delicate stemware. He disappeared into the kitchen and set about clattering plates.

"You were right," Chloe whispered. "Not eccentric, but an out and out certifiable freaking weirdo. Do you think the food's safe to eat?"

Hans grinned. "You think the meat's from previous visitors? Slaughtered in their beds and minced for the next guests?" He made Norman Bates slasher motions.

"Stop it. That's not funny. The guy gives me the heebie-jeebies."

"Come on, Chloe. You can't expect a full menu if there's no other guests. It's not like we made reservations or anything. Guy's doing his best. The table looks nice, right?"

"I suppose."

Louie returned bearing two enormous platters of steaming lasagna and crisp salad, and a basket of fragrant garlic bread. "Enjoy."

"Are we your only guests?" Hans asked.

"Until the umpire arrives tomorrow," Louie said.

"Why don't you pull up a chair and join us? Tell us a bit about yourself."

"I wouldn't want to spoil your romantic evening."

"Nonsense," Hans said. "We'd love to know more about the history of this place, wouldn't we?"

Chloe kicked Hans under the table and smiled sweetly at Louie. "Join us, please. Are you having lasagna, too?"

"If you're sure, I'll fetch my plate. Not had company for a while." Louie snagged a chair while Hans and Chloe shuffled to make room.

Louie returned with his dinner and a tankard of golden liquid.

"Have you been here long?" Hans asked. "Must get lonely."

Louie forked a generous mouthful and chewed carefully. "Coming up on twenty-five years. That's the purpose of the snap competition. Need a new Snapper King to replace me."

"Will the competitors arrive tomorrow? With the umpire? Is that why you removed the sign?" Chloe asked.

"Ever see that Kevin Costner film? Build it and they'll come, or some such nonsense. No, you gotta advertise." Louie leered. "You're here now, so I don't need the banner."

"But we're not here to compete," Chloe said. "We got lost and our van broke down. We don't play."

Louie winked. "Of course you do. Everyone competes, even though most of the time they don't know they're playing. I had no idea what I was doing when I arrived. Lost the game, haven't left the property since, but my time is almost up. I only need to find a willing replacement."

"What's a Snapper King?" Hans asked. "What's the prize?"

Louie mopped up the gooey tomatoey remains with a crust of garlic bread. "We crown the loser Snapper King, the winner walks free."

"If you don't offer a real prize," Chloe said, "I can see why you don't attract any competitors. It's not like this place is easy to find, either."

"You found your way," Louie said. "In my experience, people value their freedom above all else."

"Speaking of freedom," Hans said, "we must find a garage or a mechanic. May we borrow your phone? There isn't one in our room."

"Not much call for phones in the rooms. There's an old Yellow Pages behind the bar, but won't do you any good. Lines are down."

Chloe dropped her fork. "For how long?"

Louie shrugged. "Hard to say. Could be hours, could be weeks. Depends on what's wrong and where. I suggest you both get a good night's sleep, ready for tomorrow's event." He gathered the plates. "Help yourselves to ice creams from the freezer by the front door if you want dessert." He shuffled into the kitchen without a further word. The kitchen lights clicked off and silence filled the restaurant.

"I don't think he's coming back," Hans said. "Fancy a Cornetto?"

Chloe and Hans tip-toed out of the pub. Night had dropped with the finality of a theatre curtain. Invisible lizards squabbled amongst the fallen eucalyptus bark and leaves, and bats screeched as they snatched unsuspecting insects out of the damp air.

The backpackers slept as only the innocent can: deeply and without the distraction or judgement of dreams. The throbbing roar of a powerful four-wheel drive roused them.

Louie, smartly attired in dress shirt and long pants, greeted them at the top of the pub steps and ushered them to a green baize table and a man dressed entirely in matte black. "May I introduce Mr Sharp, our umpire?"

Mr Sharp rose to an impressive height of nearly seven feet. He bowed and offered a hand to Chloe. "Enchanted, mademoiselle." He looked Hans up and down. "Mondamoiseau, my old friend Louie informs me you are the Snapper King challenger. Do you enter freely of your own choice? Without being compelled against your will?"

Hans shrugged. "I guess it'll pass the time until the phone lines are reconnected."

"Good enough." Mr Sharp slipped off his jacket and hung it on the back of his chair. He produced a fresh packet of playing cards and removed the cellophane wrapper, which he meticulous-ly folded and put back in his pocket. "One cannot be too careful disposing of litter, yes?"

"A warm up game first? To get your eye in?" Louie asked.

"I haven't played Snap since I was, what? Seven?"

"Don't do this," Chloe said. "Nothing about this situation feels right."

Hans wrapped his arm around her waist and pulled her close. "Relax. It's a harmless bit of fun, a kids' game. I used to be good at this."

Chloe pulled away and moved behind his chair.

Mr Sharp removed the Jokers. He expertly shuffled and dealt twenty-six cards to each player. "Youngest player goes first." He nodded to Hans.

Slap.

Slap.

Slap.

Slap.

"Snap!" Hans collected the small stack and placed the cards beneath his existing pile. "Are we playing winner takes all, or are we against the clock?"

"We have all the time in the world," Mr Sharp said. "I favour a winner takes all scenario. You are ready to play for real, yes?"

Hans grinned. "Let's do this. I'd forgotten how much fun this is."

Mr Sharp collected the cards and swapped them for another sealed packet. He re-enacted his ritual as he smiled at Hans. "Your last chance to back out. No?"

"Deal!" Hans slapped the table, excited as his schoolboy self.

Chloe backed away to the bar where she wouldn't have to watch, and perched on a stool before the vintage wall-mounted rotary telephone. She paged through the out-of-date phone directory. None of the place names were familiar. All sounded as though they were concocted by inebriated Scrabble players who stammered. She lifted the old plastic handset and jiggled the hook switch. "Hello?" Silence. She slammed down the receiver, certain someone, or something, was listening.

The gamers fevered slapping and snapping abraded Chloe's already fraught nerves. She helped herself to a bottle of water and wandered outside to sit on the sagging steps. The scent of eucalyptus calmed her while she concentrated on the line of green ants carrying who knew what back to their nest, each creature utterly absorbed in their task, assured of their place in the hierarchy. A gentle breeze tempered the sun's ferocity. Chloe dozed under the timeless dappled light.

Shadows had shifted when Hans plunked down beside her. A rueful smile played on his lips. "I lost."

"Can we cadge a lift from Mr Sharp? The phone's still out of order." Chloe shivered. "We'll hire another vehicle in the next town. I just want to go. Now."

"We can't leave."

"Of course we can. Pay the bill and we'll hitch a lift with Sharp. I'll walk if I must, but I'm not staying here another night."

"Sharp's already gone. I'm surprised you didn't hear him leave in that beast of a vehicle."

Single bag in hand, Louie danced down the steps and slid behind the wheel of Klara, the clapped out Kombi. The engine purred to life and Louie lurched down the rutted path in the resurrected vehicle.

"Is this some kind of joke?"

Hans stood and pulled Chloe to her feet. "Walk with me."

They followed the overgrown track Louie had taken. Kookaburras screamed with laughter as they tramped past the bend. The dilapidated pub rose before them.

"I'm sorry." Hans' words were dust. "I tried before I woke you. I didn't believe Louie or Mr Sharp, but it's true. We can't leave. Not until we serve our quarter century and lure some poor, gullible fool to take our place."

Chloe stormed down the path, determined to discover how the ridiculous trick worked. She jogged past the bend and found herself once again facing the pub entrance, where Hans waited with glowing eyes to welcome her home.

Meet Sam Woodgarth, a retired teacher who spends her days wrangling cats and talking to her imaginary friends. No, you didn't misread that. But don't worry, she's not crazy, just a creative soul who grew up immersed in storybooks.

Sam was devastated when she realised reality didn't match the fictional worlds she read about. So, she did what any sane person would: she created her own worlds where the good guys always win, and the bad guys get their just desserts. Flambé style.

She's all about courage, honour, and wisdom, and she refuses to accept a world where fear, selfishness, and idiocy rule the day. Sam writes stories that speak to the unloved and dispossessed. Social justice is the lifeblood of her work. She's all about belonging and compassion, and she believes that we're one step closer to creating a better world if we can imagine a place where gender, religion, ethnicity, and age are accepted without question.

Originally from rainy Manchester, UK, Sam moved to Cairns, Far North Queensland, in search of her tribe. She found them in her writers' group, where she champions fellow authors and helps them find their authentic voices.

If you enjoy Sam's work, please leave a review.

Please note Sam uses UK spelling as a style choice.

Use the QR code to visit her website and sign up for her newsletter for (almost) regular updates.

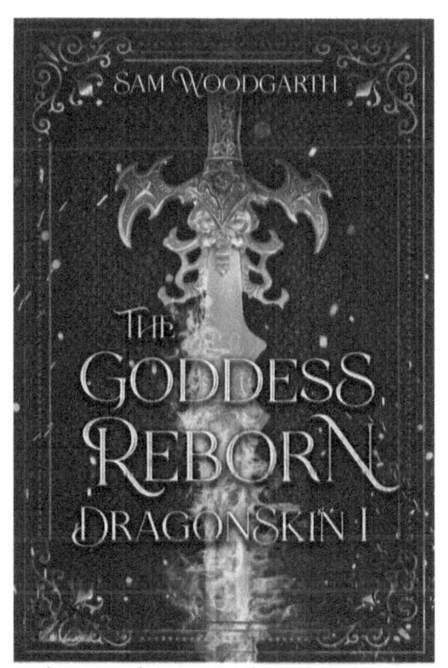

The Goddess Reborn Dragon-Skin I

If you enjoy feminist fantasy where women display strength, bravery, and loyalty in epic adventures, whose friendship and empowerment lead to

triumph and self discovery, you'll love The Goddess Reborn DragonSkin I.

Meet Annie, a reluctant heroine, who seeks independence and rewrites her destiny

Fantastical whispers thread through the festival crowd. Are the rumours true? Southern deserts turned to glass? Northern cattle herds snap frozen?

The unthinkable is compounded by the impossible. Annie Weaver is ambushed by rogue slave traders and rescued by a telepathic dragon who claims Annie is an incarnation of the missing Creator Goddess.

Annie believes in neither dragons nor deities and is forced to assess reality.

To enjoy a fast-paced action fantasy populated with quirky characters and unique fantasy creatures, check out

The Goddess Reborn DragonSkin I.

https://books2read.com/The-Goddess-Reborn

For fans of "*The Name of The Wind*" by Patrick Rothfuss and "*The Bone Shard Daughter*" by Andrea Stewart.

Restoration DragonSkin II

Older than time. More resolute than Mountains. A Darkness stirs, creating a flaw in the tapestry of creation only AnnieRah, the Goddess Reborn, can see.

No good deed goes unpunished. Annie has unwittingly summoned the ancient Dark Lord, whose very existence is a danger to the survival of all life.

After eons of plotting, the malevolent Most High Lord Draqshet unleashes demons in a diabolical bid for supremacy. Unaware of their true identities and desperate to secure favour, his servants clash with their own kin. Contemptuous of all life, Draqshet's sorcery will crush the feeble and install a hierarchy of hatred.

Rebellion brews within Annie's inner circle, testing the strength of friendship. She must forge strange new alliances and navigate a path of truth through a thicket of treachery to triumph over the Most High Lord Draqshet.

Lines blur between friends and foes. A demon's quest for independence solves an ancient mystery and leaves to self-discovery and redemption.

Fans of the mythic evil in Lim's "*Six Crimson Cranes*", and Anderson's expansive "*The Mistborn Saga*" will love Woodgarth's DragonSkin series.

Isle of The Immortals DragonSkin III

An epic fantasy adventure set in an alternative world of tropical mystery, enchantment, and unique sea dragon lore.

Lady Amora commissions a ship crafted from ancient sea dragon bones. Accompanied by loyal companions and a hastily assembled crew, she embarks on an expedition to uncharted realms.

Baptised by salt water, the newly sentient ship yearns for freedom. Once ruler of the oceans with mythical powers, but now bound in servitude, she experiences homicidal urges.

Cast into shark infested waters, Lady Amora vows vengeance against the renegade ship.

She is rescued by a tribe with access to a miraculous substance, Bounty, which confers near immortality, and is seduced by their idyllic tropical lifestyle.

Until she discovers Bounty's horrific side effects.

When the Sea dragon bone ship falls prey to the nightmare consequences of unlimited exposure to Bounty, Lady Amora has the opportunity to exact revenge or rehabilitate the one who tried to kill her.

Prepare to be enthralled by this gripping fantasy adventure, a must-read for fans of Robin Hobbs "Liveship Traders" and Tim Powers' "On Stranger Tides". Brace yourself for a journey that will chill your bones and ignite your imagination.

The Curse of Argendarria

Gilded cages are still prisons.

Edelia is a coveted asset with extraordinary gifts of clairvoyance, clairsentience, and clairaudience. Entangled in a skein of cruel lies, she uses her psychic skills to elevate the wealth and prestige of her malevolent guardian, the Duke of Bruta Rex.

To consolidate ownership of his asset, the Duke intends to wed his ward.

Her only hope for freedom lies in reclaiming her stolen Chain of Life.

With only thirty-six days before her quadranscentennial birthday, Edelia performs a daring escape and embarks on a perilous quest to rewrite her destiny.

Pursued by a rogue Clair with a hidden agenda, she navigates a world of magic and intrigue, determined to find liberation on the mythical Isle of Argendarria.

Fans of "The Bone Season" by Samantha Shannon, "Truthwitch" by Susan Dennard, and "Graceling" by Kristin Cashore will love "The Curse of Argendarria" with its themes of strong women, magical abilities, a quest for freedom, and a richly built fantasy world.

Naïve Acolyte Castian is summarily judged, excommunicated ,and sentenced to death. He awakens in a strange place he believes to be a test from his god, Solra. Far from his familiar world of orthodox dogma and unquestioning obedience, the bizarre realities and horrifyingly advanced technologies he encounters on the fabled Isle of Nefas push Castian into a crisis of belief.

Meanwhile, the sinister High Shepherd Stark pursues unholy political ambitions while concealing a dark personal secret. As Stark's elaborate plans for total domination unfold, rebellion against the oppressive regime grows.

Amidst the brutal chaos, a fragmented resistance fights to protect the innocent and expose the truth. With experimental gadgets, hidden identities, and desperate battles, the fate of the Domains hinges on Castian awakening to the true nature of his world.

Will the resistance "bring the light", or will the darkness of the past consume them all?

Children of Solra: The Dark Underbelly of a Golden Theocracy is a gripping tale of belief, rebellion, and the quest for truth in a world where nothing is as it seems.